DRAW YOU NEAR

BOOKS BY JAN THOMPSON

CITY/COASTAL/BEACH ROMANCE

Seaside Chapel (7 Books)

JanThompson.com/seaside

Savannah Sweethearts (12 Books)

JanThompson.com/savannah

Vacation Sweethearts (8 Books)

JanThompson.com/vacation

ROMANTIC SUSPENSE/THRILLERS

Protector Sweethearts (6 Books)

JanThompson.com/protector

Defender Sweethearts (6 Books)

JanThompson.com/defender

Binary Hackers (4 Books)

JanThompson.com/binary

JanThompson.com/books

DRAW YOU NEAR

SAVANNAH SWEETHEARTS
BOOK FOUR

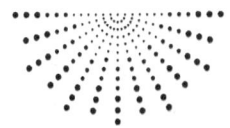

JAN THOMPSON

GEORGIA
PRESS

DRAW YOU NEAR (SAVANNAH
SWEETHEARTS BOOK 4)

Book News: JanThompson.com/newsletter
Author Website: JanThompson.com
Published by Georgia Press LLC

eBook Cover Design: Georgia Press LLC
Paperback Cover Design: Georgia Press and Deranged Doctor
Design

ISBN 978-1-944188-03-0
Paperback ISBN 978-1-944188-28-3

To my Lord and Savior, Jesus Christ, who died on the cross to save me from my sins and rose again from the grave to give me eternal life in heaven.

For God so loved the world that He gave His only begotten Son, that whoever believes in Him should not perish but have everlasting life.
—John 3:16

READ A FREE EBOOK IN THE SAME STORY WORLD

Set in Georgia, South Carolina, and Tennessee, this clean and wholesome Christian romance tells the story of art gallery archivist Sheryl Breckenridge and world-famous sculptor Winton Pace. Read this ebook for free!

Time for Me (A Vacation Sweethearts Prequel)
JanThompson.com/time-free

ABOUT THE SAVANNAH SWEETHEARTS SERIES

From *USA Today* bestselling author Jan Thompson come these clean and wholesome Christian romances set on the romantic beaches of Tybee Island and in the coastal city of Savannah, Georgia, two of the most romantic coastal towns in the world.

Against a backdrop of ocean, sand, and sun, these inspirational stories showcase aspects of the human need for God and for one another. Have some tea, settle in a comfortable reading chair, and enjoy these celebrations of faith, hope, and love in Jesus Christ.

SAVANNAH SWEETHEARTS

- Book 1: Ask You Later
- Book 2: Know You More

- Book 3: Tell You Soon
- Book 4: Draw You Near
- Book 5: Cherish You So
- Book 6: Walk You There
- Book 7: Love You Always
- Book 8: Kiss You Now
- Book 9: Find You Again
- Book 10: Wish You Joy
- Book 11: Call You Home
- Book 12: Let You Go

While Savannah Sweethearts books can be read as standalone stories, you can see a bigger picture of the Riverside Chapel community and get a glimpse of the futures of previous characters if you read Books 1-12 in order.

Savannah Sweethearts:
JanThompson.com/sweethearts

For book news, sign up for Jan's mailing list:
JanThompson.com/newsletter

YOU ARE READING DRAW YOU NEAR

SAVANNAH SWEETHEARTS BOOK 4

*Lars and Abilene are drawn to each other,
but will their relationship end up
like an unfinished painting?*

Savannah artist Abilene Dupree keeps her personal life out of her commercial paintings except one. That one painting has now brought Londoner Lars Tabansi Cargill back to the coastal town and into her art world.

Can she hold him at bay before he invades her personal space and paints his way into her heart?

LARS'S LABOR...

While on vacation in Savannah last year, Lars Cargill bought a small watercolor painting for his estate in England. The more he stared at the artwork, the more he wanted to meet the woman in the painting.

This summer, Lars returns to Savannah to find the elusive real-life Lady and the Sea. Problem is, the artist says she doesn't exist.

Of course, he doesn't believe her. Otherwise, he wouldn't be showing up in her art classes and following her around. He doubts she has the heart to turn him away, not when he shows her that he has artistic potential.

ABILENE'S ART...

Abilene Dupree is busy trying to make a living as an artist and art teacher in Savannah.

She sells commercial art, not personal stories. Although much of her heart goes into her paintings, she doesn't reveal her soul, not even to the clean-cut guy with cute dimples who is searching for the woman in her Lady and the Sea painting.

She keeps telling Lars that the elusive and illusive woman in the painting doesn't exist.

Well, the more she tells him that, the more she begins to believe her own words.

Before she can give him the real answers he seeks, Lars's own past shows up and he has to leave Savannah.

Lars and Abilene are drawn to each other, but will their relationship end up like an unfinished painting?

Draw You Near (Savannah Sweethearts Book 4):
JanThompson.com/draw

Savannah Sweethearts:
JanThompson.com/savannah

For book news, sign up for Jan's mailing list:
JanThompson.com/newsletter

DRAW YOU NEAR

CHAPTER ONE

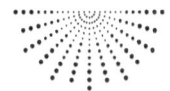

*S*unrise was Abilene Dupree's favorite morning hour at the Savannah waterfront.

With River Street still deserted behind her, the Savannah River uncrowded in front of her save for a tall ship and a couple of riverboats, she had a clear view of the May sunrise coming across the sky to her right, casting golden hues on the Talmadge Memorial Bridge to her left, spanning the river to Hutchinson Island on the other side.

Abilene strolled along the river, her easel backpack slung over her shoulders and her oil-paper carrier hanging over an arm, as she sipped hot Starbucks in a ceramic travel mug that an ex-boyfriend had personalized for her.

Past the Rousakis Riverfront Plaza, the second

riverboat waited for Abilene. It was smaller than the other.

She found a spot where the morning sun would shine on the riverboat when she painted. She put down her mug and set up her easel.

The dry paper clipped into place, she picked through her tubes of paint, squeezing them onto her palette while humming a hymn from the church service the Sunday before.

Around her, joggers and walkers went about their quiet business. Some tourists stopped to watch Abilene paint.

She was used to it. She just smiled for the camera, waved, and went back to work. Southern charm and all that.

Sure, she was a transplant from New Orleans, but she'd considered Savannah her home for the past ten years.

She was thanking God for the beautiful day that the Lord had made, when something between her easel and the riverboat caught her eye.

A vision in blue.

Blue shirt, blue cargo shorts.

Oh no.

He walked toward her, two paper cups in his hands. He was tall and fit and buff, but unwelcomed.

"Good morning!"

His British voice, tinged with a faint accent of some sort, was pleasant, she'd give him that.

"You again." Abilene frowned. She'd been frowning all week whenever Lars Tabansi Cargill showed up.

"Me again." The more he smiled, the more his dimples deepened.

His short hair combed down and wet said that he had just gotten out of the shower. But his five o'clock shadow said he hadn't bothered to shave.

Abilene knew Lars was staying at a hotel here on River Street, because he'd told her. He had also told her many other things she didn't want to hear and had asked her questions she didn't want to answer.

"I brought coffee." He offered her one of the cups.

"No, thanks." She pointed to her travel mug on the ground. "I have my own."

"But this is hazelnut, your favorite, isn't it?"

"Not today." He knew too much about her since their first conversation at Simon's Gallery.

A visitor in town, Lars had been pestering her for a week to reveal the identity of the woman in the painting he had bought from Simon's Gallery a year before.

He had come all the way here from London just to find her. Not Abilene the painter, but the woman in her painting, sitting on a beach chair on Tybee Island.

Abilene remembered that watercolor painting vividly, but she didn't want to talk about it.

"I thought you went home." She dabbed her brush into more paint. She kept moving the brush, hoping that if she looked busy, he'd go away.

"What's another week?" Lars stepped closer.

"Don't you have to work?"

"I'm in between jobs."

"In other words, you're unemployed."

"Self-employed." He fished for a piece of paper from his pocket. Unfolded it.

Abilene rolled her eyes. "No."

"Yes. I need a name." Lars held the paper up. It was a color copy of the painting that had besotted the Londoner. "Give me a name, and I'll be out of your hair."

That was the thing! Lars wanted her to tell him the history of the painting. She wanted him to be history. "Go home, Lars. There's nothing to tell."

"I'll pay you anything. I want to meet this woman."

"It's just a painting, Lars. Nothing more." Not for him to know, anyway.

"I don't believe you."

"Yeah, you said that last week."

"I asked Simon. He doesn't know."

"No, he doesn't. He just shows my artwork."

Lars opened his mouth to speak just as his phone rang.

"Here, hold this." He handed Abilene one of the coffee cups. "Better drink it before it gets cold."

~

"*W*hen are you coming home, Lars?"

"Are you checking up on me?" Lars walked briskly away from Abilene and hoped she couldn't hear the conversation. Somehow he found himself heading toward the riverboat she was painting.

"Have you thought about my proposal?"

"Well, still thinking about it." Not really. Truth be told, Lars wasn't sure he wanted to work at Cargill Internet Communications, family business or not. It seemed dull and uninspiring.

"How long are you going to be in America?" Colm pressed.

"Maybe through the summer. Why?"

"Just wondering."

In his heart, Lars felt good that his brother called. They hadn't spoken in over a week. However, he wondered if Colm would understand what he was doing in Savannah. He would probably call it a silly phase.

Lars stopped at the foot of the ramp leading up to the riverboat. He faced a stand with a clear acrylic box attached. On the box were the words *Riverside Chapel*. Inside were flyers with pictures of the riverboat. The flyers looked somewhat familiar.

He glanced behind his shoulder to find Abilene in the distance waving for him to step aside. He waved back but didn't move. He doubted he was really getting in her way. Well, she could paint around him.

"Summer is a long time, Lars." Colm's voice was deeper than Lars's, but if they were standing side by side, they could pass for fraternal twins.

Only fourteen months apart, they had been inseparable until they went off to different universities. While Colm had chosen to stay closer to home, Lars had gone off to Yale instead. So much for all that money spent. He hadn't done a thing with his MBA.

"You don't need me, Colm." His brother's Oxford degree had served the Cargill empire well.

"No, but since Mom passed away, you're my responsibility."

"Nope, Colm. I can take care of myself."

"Sure. Pushing thirty and not being certain of what you want to do with the rest of your life."

"That's why I'm here. I'm figuring it out."

"In Savannah."

"Yes."

"And it'll take all summer."

"Yes."

Silence.

Lars wondered what Colm was thinking over there in his glass tower.

Still standing in front of the information box, Lars opened the lid and picked up a flyer.

Yep. It was her handiwork. Lars would recognize it anywhere.

Even as he stared at the flyer, his conversation with his brother continued to play in his mind.

"Can't just live off your trust fund, you know."

"Right."

"Can't drift, Lars. You need an anchor."

An anchor? Sure. I'll find an anchor.

Staring at the flyer, Lars decided he would go to church.

CHAPTER TWO

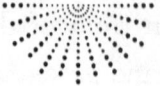

*a*bilene watched Lars kick the ground in front of the riverboat. Something seemed off, but what was it? Well, why should she care at all?

She sighed.

For one thing, Lars had some issues, right? He'd flown all the way from London just to ask her about her painting. Why couldn't he have emailed or called Simon's Gallery? Could've saved him his plane ticket and hotel expenses.

After all, he'd bought only one of the several small editions of the painting.

She had the five-by-seven original in her apartment.

There must've been a deeper need in Lars. Perhaps it wasn't the painting per se. Perhaps he was searching for something deeper in life. Why now? Why here?

Really, it wasn't her place to know. She wasn't a psychologist or a counselor. But Lars had reached out to her. Why her? Why not some other artist? Someone else?

Maybe she should introduce him to Pastor Flores—

No.

Lars should just go home. Leave town. Leave her alone. She didn't want to have anything to do with him. As long as he kept asking her about that painting, there was nothing more to say between them, regardless of his spiritual needs.

If he had any.

Well, Mr. Needy was walking toward her again.

"Like your coffee?" he asked.

"Sorry. Didn't drink it."

"You're mean."

"What?"

"I bought you coffee. You wasted it."

"I didn't ask you to buy the coffee. You wasted your own money being presumptuous."

Lars didn't say anything. In fact, his shoulders had slumped. Who had he been talking to? Why was the conversation such a downer? Abilene's curiosity had the better of her. She opened her mouth and regretted it immediately.

"Bad news?" It was all she said, but she had cracked a door she couldn't shut.

"No. Why?"

"You're slouching."

"Slouching?"

"Didn't your mother tell you to stand up straight? Shoulders back, chest out?"

"Mother died last year."

"Oh." Abilene's brush froze midway across the white ramp on her painting. "I'm sorry."

"It was cancer. Inoperable. She wanted to be buried in her homeland. It was the longest journey of my life to Botswana."

"Is Tabansi a Botswana name, then?" It was on the business card he'd given to Abilene when they'd first met a week ago.

"My grandfather's name."

Grandfather. Abilene blinked. "My grandfather also died of cancer. Six years ago now. We all mourned for months, maybe years. It's hard, but with God's help, we go on."

Lars nodded. "Only with God."

"You believe?"

"Jesus Christ is my Lord and Savior."

"Me too." Wow. A believer. "I saw you pick up a flyer over there for Riverside Chapel."

"It's a pretty flyer. Has your signature all over it."

"And you can tell?"

"Sure. I studied all your paintings." Lars suddenly looked uncomfortable. "I mean... I don't know what I mean."

"Hey, I'm flattered. Nice to have *one* fan."

"Who has more time than he knows what to do with?" Lars laughed. "Seriously, I'm sure I'm not the only one who likes your work. Something about your paintings. They linger long in my mind after I've seen them."

Abilene couldn't believe what she was hearing. "I appreciate that compliment. May I quote you?"

"Sure. It's the truth." Lars walked around the easel and stared at the painting. "You painted me into the picture?"

"I waved to you to get out of the way."

"You could've painted around me."

"I paint what's in front of me."

"Is that so?" Lars stood close enough for Abilene to smell his aftershave. It was fresh and almost lavender—huh?—but it was probably her olfactory imagination running amok. Maybe it was due to a good-looking guy standing in front of her. Were they all this charming? Someday she wanted to go to Britain and paint the countryside. The Cotswolds. Bibury. Oxford.

Someday.

"Do I get to sign the painting if I'm in it?"

Huh? "No, sir. I'm the artist here. You just got in the way."

"I see. I'm a fly on the wall."

Abilene laughed. "So fly away."

Lars didn't move. "You're really good at this art thing."

Art thing? "I enjoy it, but it's hard work."

"You make it look easy."

"Painting is easy. Selling paintings is not easy."

"Is that right?"

Abilene tipped her head. "There's a reason we're called starving artists."

"You're starving? Let me buy you lunch."

"Silly pickle, you know what I mean."

"No one has ever called me a silly pickle before."

Abilene didn't apologize.

"You can call me anything you want." Lars smiled.

"A pain in the neck?"

"Am I? Do I bother you that much?"

Yes and yes. But Abilene didn't say it. There was pain in his eyes. A loss? A regret? She decided she had to be careful of what she said to him. Sure, he was a pest. He'd been a pest all week, asking about that painting. She didn't have to give him an answer. An artist never had to reveal everything.

Still, there he was.

What if God had brought him here for such a time as this?

Such a time as what?

"Are you painting all day?" Lars asked, changing the subject.

Just as well, Abilene thought. She had no solution, no breakthrough here. She wanted to be left alone.

"I have to finish this painting today," Abilene declared, partly to tell Lars it was time to move on, and partly to avoid having to deal with him.

"I thought artists work with their own deadlines."

"Sometimes. If it's a commissioned work, there's always outside pressure to finish the work. Classes and such also have schedules that I sometimes can't change."

Lars threw out the cups of cold coffee into a nearby trash can. He came back. "I need a hobby. Do you think painting is therapeutic?"

Abilene wondered why he asked that.

Oh well. No point reading too much into it. She decided to take the question at face value, the way she'd take it if one of her art students had asked.

"I think any art form can be therapeutic. Playing a musical instrument, listening to music, and of course, drawing, painting, reading. Anything fun and relaxing can be therapeutic."

"I'm thinking of taking up art. Is it too late to learn?"

"It's never too late to learn. What were you thinking of? Sketching? Pencil? Oil? Acrylic? Watercolor?"

Lars seemed to be lost in thought. Then: "Your *Lady and the Sea* painting is in watercolor."

"Yes."

"That riverboat is in oil."

"Good observation." Abilene kept on painting. Last bits left.

She decided not to go back and touch up the sky. It had been a deeper blue when she started the painting, and that was the way it went. This morning's sky was a lighter hue of blue, but she decided the French blue went better with the white riverboat.

The blue in her painting matched Lars's blue shirt.

Abilene wondered why she even noticed, but it wasn't like her to psychoanalyze herself. She'd rather let life flow the way it flowed.

Right now it was flowing around Lars, flooding her morning with mixed feelings.

Maybe she should answer his questions about the painting, if only to send him on his merry way.

Well, if he would just leave her alone, then she wouldn't have to answer any question at all or think about the past and present and future and whatever else swirled around that *Lady and the Sea* painting.

Lars dipped his hand into his cargo shorts pocket. Abilene heard crinkling paper. That paper.

"It's a composite," she finally said. "I painted it on a whim, sitting on the beach."

"On a whim?"

"Uh-huh."

"No particular woman in mind?"

"Just my overactive imagination. Now you can go home. Find a real person. Not a painting."

Lars nodded. "Thank you for your time, Abilene Dupree. Nice to meet you."

"Have a good life, okay?"

"You too."

Abilene watched him go, slumped shoulders, invisible burdens, and all.

Whew. It was nice to get her space back. She cleaned off a brush, dipped it into red paint, and was about to highlight the waterwheel at the back of the riverboat, when her eyes went to the man in her painting, standing there reading a flyer in front of the ramp.

Why on earth had she painted him into her scene?

CHAPTER THREE

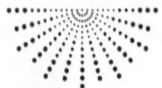

*U*nbelievable. He actually showed up in church.

Abilene pretended not to see Lars coming up the ramp outside the riverboat. She kept on handing out sheets of the Sunday morning program to regular churchgoers entering the dining room on the top deck of the riverboat. She hoped there was a time gap between the crowd she was greeting and Lars reaching the door so that she could put down the stack of programs and sit down.

Hadn't she told him to go home? Get a life or something?

Here he was in church.

Her church.

Of all the many churches in Savannah, and some were historic and dated all the way back to the city's colonial days, Lars had to choose this church. This one!

God, please could you send him away?

Abilene spotted her friend coming down the hallway. She motioned for Nadine to hurry.

"Whassup?" Nadine crossed the pine floorboards, her chunky heels color-matching Abilene's. They'd saved up for months, then bought those pumps at the same time. It put Abilene out a few hundred dollars, but she knew the shoes would last.

Abilene thrust the stack of programs into her friend's hands. "Take these. I have to go to the girls' room."

"Without a *pretty please?*"

"Please. I beg you. Have to go." Abilene was halfway there when she spotted the vision of gray at the corner of her left eye. She could say, from an artistic viewpoint, that he looked good in the gray oxford shirt and charcoal slacks.

She closed the ladies' room door behind her and sat down on the upholstered bench next to an ornate mirror. She held her chest.

What's going on?

Why was she nervous all of a sudden? Lots of people went to church. They all needed Jesus, including Lars.

Including Lars.

~

*L*ars knew that had been Abilene walking away from him, heading for the ladies' restroom. He counted the minutes as he sat at the back of the dining room, waiting for church to start, reading the Sunday program over and over, tapping the table with his fingers.

He was sure no one paid any attention to him. They were talking among themselves.

Shortly after, other people came in.

"Is this seat taken?" An elderly gentleman pointed to the empty seat next to Lars.

"Yours." Lars smiled.

The couple sat down and introduced themselves. Lars glanced back every chance he had. He didn't know why. Abilene had all but told him to go home.

Well, he was working on that.

The lady at the grand piano started to play a few quiet hymns, some of which Lars had heard before while attending his mother's church. He hadn't been back since she passed away last summer. The Cargill family continued to attend there, but Lars had felt no connection to the past after Mother went to heaven.

Truly, he couldn't go back to their family church. Every time he had stood in the sanctuary, his mind was flooded with memories of Mother holding his hand when he was a little boy in his Sunday best.

Outside the riverboat, the sun was up. Sunday tourists dotted the waterfront. The spot where Abilene had been the day before was now unoccupied.

Lars remembered how she had added him to the painting because he had stood in front of her subject. She didn't seem to be the kind who might do such an improvisation as that.

He had misjudged her. He'd thought all her paintings had been thoughtful and planned. Apparently some were not.

Perhaps he would never find that woman in Abilene's painting.

What would Mother have said about his falling in love with an illusion?

An ensemble began to sing and play guitars. An arrangement of Cindy Berry's "By the Gentle Waters" came through clearly on the overhead speakers.

Lars liked the feel of the room, the lack of gilded edges, the straight lines of the furnishings, the woodsy decor. Oak, he presumed. Perhaps oak from this area. Or not. The riverboat itself had been built in the seventies, a little fact he'd picked up reading about Riverside Chapel on its website.

Apparently Pastor Diego Flores had friends, one of whom was an elderly riverboat owner who had gotten saved and decided not to work on Sundays anymore. He had loaned the riverboat for free to Riverside Chapel for Sunday services when the church's storefront lease was up.

Lars's eyes rose to the ceiling, where rows of old-world chandeliers harkened back to the twenties, a throwback design that went well with the clean lines in the dining room. His eyes followed the patterns of round tables until they reached back to the ensemble, who had just finished singing.

When everyone stood up to sing and greet one another, Lars found Abilene with her friend Nadine, whom he'd met at the door. He waited until he thought Abilene could see him.

He waved. She ignored him. Perhaps she didn't see him. No worries. He'd catch her later.

Lars liked Pastor Flores. He was not much older than the photograph on the church website. Perhaps in his late twenties or early thirties.

"You've heard Shakespeare say, 'To thine own self be true,' haven't you?" Pastor Flores began his sermon. "But I say to you, to God be true. See yourself the way God sees you. He is the way, the truth, the life. Let's turn to John 14:6 and read that together."

Lars followed along on his iPhone.

Jesus said to him, "I am the way, the truth, and the life. No one comes to the Father except through Me."

The truth.
Exactly what Lars wanted.

CHAPTER FOUR

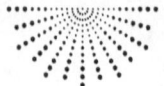

*B*efore Abilene knew it, church was over. She didn't see Lars. She wasn't sure why it bothered her, really. She had told him the woman in the painting was a random composite. His quest had come to an end. He might as well check out of the hotel and fly home to London.

And yet...

Abilene chided herself for not paying attention after they'd sung the last hymn and Pastor Flores had given the invitation. She found herself being dragged from her seat by the overcaffeinated Nadine, pushing her way through the crowd filing out of the dining room.

They stopped right at the door, where Pastor Diego Flores was shaking hands with some people.

Visitors had been going through Riverside

Chapel since it had started holding Sunday morning services on the riverboat the summer before. Some had attended services out of curiosity and thought it a novelty to get their pictures taken on a floating church. Others came to fill genuine spiritual needs. Sometimes residents of Savannah and the surrounding areas showed up to consider Riverside Chapel for a church home.

Whatever the reason, Abilene knew all ninety-four members of the church were happy they were still going after these months on their new riverboat location.

Standing next to Pastor Flores, Heidi Wei-Flores handed out visitor cards. She had been one of the earliest members of the newly reconstructed church, and had known her husband some years before he came to Savannah to take over the church leadership.

Riverside Chapel had come a long way, a remnant or splinter from a bigger church that had shut down. Its growth had been spurred on by the tireless efforts of Heidi, her brother, Aidan Ming Wei, and other charter members, such as Roger Patel and Camden La Salle. Well, Nadine and Abilene had been in that early church group too.

It had been, and was still, a group effort to grow a church from hardly anything.

Speaking of Ming, where were he and his wife, Sabine?

Abilene was so busy looking for Ming and Sabine that she missed the tall apparition in front of her. Only it wasn't an apparition or a shadow blocking the ceiling lights. It was Lars, and he had shaven nicely.

"Hello, Abilene."

Abilene put on her cheery self. "I thought you went home."

"Soon."

"When?"

Lars shrugged.

Nadine cut in front of Abilene. "Ignore my friend. She's kidding. We welcome visitors to our church."

"I might not be a visitor much longer. I just asked your pastor for membership." Lars was all smiles.

"What?" Abilene frowned. "You can't—"

"I'm a believer too, remember?"

"You don't live in the United States."

"Well, Savannah could be my second home."

"You're going to move here?"

"Does that bother you?" He was standing very close. Close enough to give Abilene another whiff of that aftershave that reminded her of the smell of a clear, crisp waterfall.

"What will you do in Savannah?"

"I don't know, Abilene. We've discussed that I don't have any useful skills, remember?"

Nadine grabbed Abilene's arm.

"Excuse us a minute, Lars." Nadine took Abilene aside, snarling as they went to a corner. She took a deep, deep breath. "Okay, Abilene. What's wrong with you, woman? PMS?"

"Huh?"

"You pitched a fit because some handsome guy asked to join our church?"

"He's in my space."

"Your space?" Nadine kept her whispers down, but Abilene could see she was going to explode. "The last time I checked, a church is God's space, not yours."

"I meant—"

"Be happy that we could—I emphasize could!— potentially have ninety-five members instead of ninety-four. That's a very long way toward the two hundred we're trying to get to fill this creaky old riverboat. Don't you want our church to grow?"

"He lives in London."

"We're an international church in a global city."

"Well—"

"I'm going to ask him out," Nadine said.

"What?" Abilene tried to keep her voice down. "You can't ask everyone out."

"Watch me." Nadine strutted away, Abilene at her heels.

Nadine went straight up to Lars. He was talking with Ming, who had appeared out of nowhere.

"Hey Lars," Nadine said. "We're going to Piper's Place for lunch. Want to come?"

"Sure."

Nadine threw Abilene a quick smile as if to say *Score!*

Abilene sighed. She noticed that Ming was alone. "Where's Sabine?"

"At home. She's not feeling well."

"So sorry. Anything we can do?" Abilene asked.

"Not much. It's morning sickness."

"Oh." Abilene was lost in thought when she heard Lars's voice close to her ear.

"Are you coming to lunch with us?" Lars's face seemed hopeful, the last thing she needed.

Us?

"Nope. I've got work to do. You guys have fun." Abilene walked alone out of the dining room and into the warm Savannah noonday.

CHAPTER FIVE

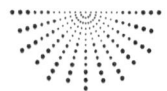

hat Nadine had said back at church now stung and put Abilene in her place.

Abilene sat alone on her little patio, eating her pimiento sandwich and chewing over Nadine's chiding. The more she thought of Nadine's chiding of her, the more her sandwich tasted stale and bitter in her mouth.

Exactly what had overcome her at church this morning to warrant such childish behavior?

Yes, she should've been glad that Lars had not only come to church this morning.

Yes, she should've been excited that Lars wanted to become a member of Riverside Chapel.

Not that his membership was automatic. Ming, the volunteer membership coordinator, would check

Lars's background, and then the church committee would discuss his request.

I'm a believer too, remember?

Lars's words put Abilene to shame. She asked God for forgiveness for her irrational behavior.

Well, he had asked too many questions. She had given him what amounted to a brush-off. An artist had to protect her craft, her subject, her livelihood. There should be a fourth wall between her and all those people buying her artwork.

Right?

Abilene put down the half-eaten sandwich on the paper plate and pushed it to one side of the bistro table. On the other wrought iron chair, her cat, Bradley, was sleeping soundly.

Beyond the small patio was an odd-shaped green space that used to be a garden of some sort. Above her, dark clouds were moving in.

She hadn't wanted to keep renting after graduating from the Savannah College of Art and Design, but she wasn't sure what she wanted to do, where she wanted to settle down. She wanted God's will for her life most of all, but for the moment she had no idea where God would lead her, only that work kept piling up in Savannah and she stayed to collect the income.

Simon's Gallery was doing well. The owner wanted to show a series of paintings on coastal

Georgia, and Abilene was still thrilled she was one of the local artists who had made the final cut. When Simon had congratulated her, he'd specifically requested a painting of Riverside Chapel.

That riverboat painting would be one of the gallery's showcase pieces. Abilene still had a few minor touch-ups to do that no one would notice but the artist herself, but once done, she knew it would bring profit to Simon's Gallery.

Tourists loved commercial art pieces like that.

Abilene cleared the table and walked back into her small one-bedroom apartment. If she had rented a two-bedroom place, she could store her art equipment in the spare room. For now, her living room inside the patio door was her art studio.

She tossed out her unfinished sandwich and popped open a can of mineral water. She walked toward a corner of the living room, where a vertical stack of paintings held court. Five so far of varying sizes. All painted this year, and it was only May.

Yeah, she didn't have a life outside art.

Every now and then Abilene would spread out those paintings, trying to finalize which originals she'd keep and which ones she would sell, never to see them again.

Possessiveness took hold of her as she lined up those paintings against the wall, the couch, the barstools, the patio door. Bradley wove in and out of the collection, some framed, some not, his striped tail brushing against the paintings as he went.

Abilene paused at the last painting in the group.

There it was. The original five by seven.

She would've painted on a bigger canvas except that she couldn't afford a frame bigger than this. All Lars had was one of the five smaller replicas she had made of the same subject.

Of all the paintings she'd sold through Simon's Gallery, Lars had to pick the *Lady and the Sea.*

Well, many people bought coastal artwork when they came to Savannah.

This painting wasn't done in Savannah per se, but at her favorite spot on Tybee Island between North Beach and Mid Beach. She would go there and sit for hours. That was her spot. Her quiet place. Her hiding place.

It was the last place she wanted to share with a total stranger she'd only known for a week or so.

And she had told Lars the truth. The woman was a composite image. She was a result of Abilene's imagination.

She didn't tell him that it was a part of a series she had planned. The next painting would be of the woman walking on the beach. Maybe she could start that today. She glanced out the patio door. The sky was overcast. Maybe not today. Sometime this week.

Her iPhone buzzed. She picked it up from the

kitchen peninsula and read the text message from Nadine.

Missing you at lunch. Lars is a hoot.

Abilene didn't reply.

~

"She's a fiercely private person." Nadine Saylor pushed the wrinkled color printout across the lunch table back toward Lars. "I'm not surprised you can't get anything out of her about this painting."

"And I'm not sure if she wants to be pestered," Ming added. "A week is a long time to persist. I'm surprised she didn't file harassment charges against you."

Lars was taken aback. "All I wanted is more information about the model. Is it too much to ask?"

"For Abilene, everything is too much to ask." Ming chuckled.

"Well, I'm not sure if I'd go that far." Nadine sounded defensive of Abilene.

Best friends? Definitely sisters in Christ.

Lars had noticed that Abilene and Nadine had color-coordinated shoes. He reminded himself to be careful what he said about Abilene in front of Nadine.

He folded the paper and pocketed it. Maybe if

he put it away, they wouldn't accuse him of harassing their friend. Really, he could've shown them the photograph on his iPhone. However, he had printed the picture onto paper for the texture and feel of it.

"I guess I'll never find out who that woman is."

"You said she told you it's a composite," Nadine said.

Lars nodded.

"Then take her word for it, and leave her alone."

"I can't leave her alone. Why didn't she come to lunch with us? Is it because of me?"

Nadine shrugged. "No idea. I'll ask her later, okay?"

"Please tell her I'm sorry." Lars did feel sorry. He wasn't sure if he wanted to, but there it was in his heart. An apology.

Maybe he shouldn't have come to Savannah at all. Now that he was here, he didn't want to leave.

Now he wanted to know Abilene Dupree more.

"Well, I'd better run." Ming played with his wristwatch. "Sabine might need me."

"Me too. Lots of work to do before the church service tonight." Nadine waved to their server.

"Do you need a ride?" Ming asked Lars.

"No, thanks. My hotel is just down the street. I might pick up some fudge on the way."

"Abilene loves—" Nadine shut up abruptly.

"Fudge?" Lars smiled. "So she likes fudge. What kind of fudge?"

"Maple—uh, forget I said anything."

"You said maple."

"I don't know what I'm talking about." Nadine's eyes were big as she counted her dollars and placed them on the check tray.

Ming laughed at the two of them as he paid his bill and left the café.

Nadine ran after him.

"Nadine! Nuts or no nuts?" Lars asked.

"Pecans! Uh-oh!" Nadine chuckled as she stumbled out the door.

Lars was alone now, thinking of one more little thing he knew about Abilene Dupree.

She liked maple fudge with pecans in it.

CHAPTER SIX

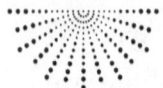

After dropping off the riverboat painting at Simon's Gallery, Abilene made her way to the water's edge by way of Starbucks.

She stood there, the early Monday morning wind brushing through her curly hair, thinking about whether to paint the Talmadge Memorial Bridge first or Hutchinson Island.

She had a good mind to add a bit of whimsy to her island painting. After all, when Savannah had been the thirteenth and last British colony in the New World, the settlers had kept herds of cows on Hutchinson Island. Perhaps a cow or two grazing in the yard of that hotel over there would catch people by surprise.

Blue cows. Maybe.

She sipped her steamy hazelnut coffee as she

surveyed the setting. Should she include those container ships in her painting of the island? The ferries too? Or should she leave the waterway bare?

She drained the last drop of coffee from her ceramic travel mug. The image screen-printed onto the mug was a cute caricature of her with her hair all frizzy and green.

Nope, she'd never had green hair, but she hadn't complained about Winton's sketch, because they had been in love. They'd met at the Savannah College of Art and Design. He was a sculptor, and she a painter. They'd been perfect together.

Now all Abilene had left of that relationship was this twenty-five-dollar travel mug.

She was about to put away the mug, when right in front of her, fresh coffee appeared, its aroma wafting into her nose and tempting her to no end.

"I won't charge you for this."

Lars.

Well, what's a desperate girl to do?

Abilene surrendered her mug to Lars Cargill. She watched him pour the entire cup of coffee—the kind she liked—from the paper cup into her mug.

He was wearing a white tee shirt with the word *Savannah* screen-printed across the chest.

"Thank you." She closed her eyes and took in the incredible fragrance that only a coffee connoisseur would understand.

"You're most welcome."

When she looked at him next, there were sparkles in Lars's eyes. And—

"Did you get a haircut?" Abilene asked.

"You like it?" Lars tipped his head this way and that.

"Nice and cropped. I didn't realize you have some wavy hair."

"A little bit of wave here and there that I got from Mother. Her hair was curly, like yours." He reached for Abilene's hair and twirled a curl in his fingers.

Abilene didn't move. His hand was too close to her face.

Lars dropped his hand. "Dad's hair was straight and wiry. It turned all white the last few years of his life."

"I'm sorry. Every time we talk about family, there are always mentions of death."

"Such is life, you know. At least both my parents were believers, and I know they're in heaven now with God."

"The best place to be," Abilene added.

"Meanwhile, we do our best on earth as long as we're still here."

"Do some good and serve God?"

Lars's gaze bore down on her. "My brother said I'm drifting through life. Do you think I'm drifting?"

"Well, I don't know you that well, Lars." Abilene started walking. It was then that she realized Lars had something else with him other than coffee.

He picked up a canvas bag, smaller than hers, from the ground, and slung it over one shoulder. She was familiar with such a bag.

What was he up to?

"Do I look like I'm drifting?" Lars tried again.

"Your brother knows you more than any one of us here does. So if he thinks you're drifting, you might want to check if you are. Maybe you did wash up on the shores of Savannah."

"Are you calling me washed up?"

"I didn't say that."

"You did too." He nudged her arm.

Abilene ignored him as she considered a spot to set up her easel. "Must be nice to have so much time to fly around and do nothing."

"I'm not doing *nothing*. I'm researching the *Lady and the Sea*. I know you said the model is a composite. I want to believe you made it up."

"Believe what you will. Can't help you there."

Lars stopped where Abilene did. She unzipped her bag, and so did he. Her eyes grew wide at what spilled out of his bag.

Lars seemed proud of himself. He put the folded-up aluminum easel on the ground and dug around in the bag for something. A booklet. He read through it. He tried to unfold the easel. Then he read the booklet again.

Abilene sighed, put down her coffee, and stepped toward him. Without a word, she snapped the easel open, locked the joints in place, and adjusted its height.

"Thank you, Abilene." Lars put away the instruction booklet and pulled out a very small square paper, maybe six inches by six. He placed it on the easel. The little piece of paper was dwarfed by all the metal around it.

Abilene set up her own easel. Her art paper was bigger. She clipped it into place.

"What are you painting?" Lars asked.

"Trying to decide between the island or the bridge." Abilene's gaze was far away.

"How about painting both?"

"I will, but which to do first?"

"Toss a coin."

"No, silly pickle. I can do better than that." Abilene drank up her coffee. "Thanks again for the coffee."

"Anytime. I can bring you free coffee every day while I'm in town."

"When do you leave?"

"Can't wait to get rid of me?" Lars took a long time selecting one out of two pencils in his box.

Abilene was amused. *Just pick one.*

He drew a circle right in the middle of his art paper.

"That's pretty good." Abilene meant it. It was almost a perfect circle.

"I'm painting an orange today."

Abilene laughed. "You came out here to draw an orange?"

"Should it be an apple?" Lars seemed serious.

Abilene didn't want to discourage talent. "Orange sounds like it would fit better in that circle you just drew."

"We'll see. I'll send it to my brother. Then he won't think I'm just idling."

"Drifting."

"That's what he said. He even suggested I find an anchor."

"Have you found it?"

"I went to church Sunday. That's a good start, isn't it?" Lars sighed.

"I suppose."

"Glad you finally agree with me on something, Abilene. Made my day."

"It's only seven thirty."

"Glorious day it will be." Lars studied his tray of paint tubes and picked up green.

"Green orange?"

"Also known as lime."

"Lime is not orange, Lars."

"It is *my* painting."

"Okay." Abilene decided not to speak further. The more she talked, the more Lars kept on. Who knew where their conversation would lead?

Better not encourage him.

CHAPTER SEVEN

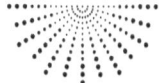

*S*he *must be in some kind of hurry.*

Lars marveled at the speed with which Abilene outlined Hutchinson Island on her art paper.

Then it was off to bright colors. She brushed in the sky so quickly that by the time he dabbed his first spot of lime green on his little painting, she was checking something on her iPhone.

Maybe she was waiting for the paint to dry.

She was beautiful in her calico summer dress with little flowers on her puffed short sleeves.

She hadn't said a word to him for the past hour. Trying to keep a Plexiglas between them?

"So. How long does it take for oil paint to dry?" Lars asked when Abilene tucked away her iPhone.

"Depends on the paint. A couple of days for some, more for others."

"You can't paint any more today, then?"

"Sure can. I'm going to paint in the grass and possibly the river before I'm done for the day."

Above them the clouds moved in.

"A gray morning, isn't it?" Lars asked. The air was a bit muggy but hotter and more humid than London.

"Probably all week," Abilene said. "Scattered thundershowers in the forecast."

"I still like it here." Sometime this week he'd rent a car and go out to Tybee Island to have a look around. He wanted to go to the spot in the *Lady and the Sea* painting.

He had shown the photograph to the concierge at the hotel, and she had told him that the North Beach on Tybee had a landscape like that somewhere south of the lighthouse. He thought maybe he could go explore.

It would be more fun if Abilene would come with him, but he'd be imposing. Besides, he didn't want her to know that he was encroaching on her beach.

Her beach?

Tybee Island wasn't hers.

"Is it easy to paint a landscape?" Lars asked.

Abilene was mixing paint. Lost in thought.

"Abilene?"

"Huh?" Abilene's eyebrows knotted.

Lars repeated his question.

"It depends on what kind of landscape. You can make it as easy or as difficult as you want."

"Art is that freeing?"

"It can be." She dabbed dark green paint everywhere on the island segments on her thick oil paper.

Lars found a brush similar to Abilene's. Mimicking her, he dabbed green all over his orange.

"Are you copying me?" Abilene asked.

"Learning from the master. That was how they did it back in Leo's days."

"Leo?"

"Leonardo da Vinci."

"Oh. Him."

"Have you seen the *Mona Lisa*?" Lars asked.

Abilene nodded. "As a matter of fact, I have. Some years ago, the Louvre loaned some paintings to the High Museum of Art in Atlanta. I went to see it when I was a student at SCAD."

"Scad?"

"Savannah College of Art and Design. SCAD."

"So I can take art classes there?"

"You can take art classes anywhere."

"Will you teach me to paint?"

"Plenty of classes in town at galleries. Take your pick."

"But you won't teach me." Lars felt disappointed.

Abilene didn't reply.

"How long have you been an artist?"

"Since I was three years old." Abilene put her brush in a plastic cup. "Why?"

"That long ago?"

"Hey, are you saying I'm old?"

Lars knew she was just kidding. "My guess is that you're about twenty-three or twenty-four years old. Am I right?"

"Are you always this direct?"

"How else do I get answers?"

"You talked to Nadine?"

"About your age?" Lars shook his head. "Nope. I can read people myself."

"And you said you have no useful skills."

"So you were listening. I have a good memory. That's all. I pick up a lot of little stuff." Lars took a deep breath. "I retract my question. It was rude of me."

"I'm twenty five." Abilene shrugged.

"You look younger."

"I'll take that as a compliment."

"It is."

"Thank you, then."

"Well, I'm almost five years older than you are. What was your first artwork?"

"Finger paint." Abilene smiled. "My parents still have that. Framed it and put it right there in their living room."

"Must be nice to have living parents."

Abilene nodded. "I didn't appreciate them as a child or as a teenager, but I do now."

"How often do you see them?"

"A few times a year."

"They live nearby?"

"Why all these questions, Lars? Go paint your orange."

"Lime orange. It's a hybrid."

"Whatever."

"Just wondering about your parents."

"They live just outside New Orleans." She couldn't say more, as the first large pelts of rain came. "Oh no! My painting is still wet."

"So what are a few more drops of rain?" Lars asked.

Abilene unclipped her paper. Holding it with the tips of her fingers in one hand, she tried to dismantle her easel with the other hand.

She couldn't do it.

"Let me." With some effort, Lars folded up the easel.

Rain drenched them before Abilene could put her art paper into her carrier.

"Get shelter." Lars bagged her easel for her. "I'll be right behind you."

Abilene pointed to the shops across the street. "I'll wait for you there."

"Go." Lars packed all her stuff and shoved it into her backpack. He zipped it up. Then he began working on his own easel.

He put both backpacks on himself, one on each shoulder. He had to wait for a taxi to pass and then a trolley before he dashed across the cobblestone road to where Abilene was standing at the door of an open store.

They were soaking wet. Abilene's hair was straightening out over her forehead and cheeks, but it still had curls in it.

Lars reached for the shock of wet curls over her face and gently eased them away from her cheekbones.

He couldn't read the expression in her eyes, but he thought that she was trying hard to fight some sort of response to his touch.

She's interested?

Maybe?

They leaned against the old brick wall outside the store. Both their backpacks were on the ground.

Abilene was holding on to her canvas of partially painted Hutchinson Island.

Lars didn't have the heart to tell her that blobs of

paint had transferred onto her palm and arms and blouse. Blue and green swirled together.

"Look at you!" Abilene exclaimed, palm to her mouth.

"What?"

"Your shirt." Abilene tried not to laugh.

The green acrylic paint had smeared off his canvas, onto his palm and hand, and then smudged his white Savannah tee shirt.

"I thought acrylic dries faster," Lars said.

"Not if you just painted it. And I try not to paint wearing a white shirt."

"A brand-new white shirt. Got it from the hotel shop over the weekend."

"Poor thing." Abilene curled her lips.

Cute.

But Lars thought it would change when she saw what had happened to her own painting. It could be ruined, for all practical purposes.

He pointed to her arm and blouse.

Abilene's big gray eyes widened. "Oh no."

"Do you have to repaint it?"

"Don't know." She held up her painting. "Maybe. Maybe not."

"I like your attitude."

Abilene didn't respond to his remark, but Lars wouldn't take it back.

He had meant it.

CHAPTER EIGHT

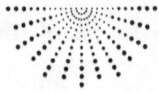

"*A*re you going to the Wednesday night Bible study?" Lars asked, sounding religious enough to make Abilene wonder if he was genuine or simply making conversation.

One of her ex-boyfriends was like that. Talking the talk and taking her to church, and then after all those niceties, she found out he didn't really believe in Jesus, only enough to get into her good graces.

Been there, done that.

But...

Lars Cargill was just passing through. A tourist, practically. He'd go home, answers or not, and then she'd never see him again.

Over the last year she had met many people at Riverside Chapel. Then they were gone. Problem with a tourist town like Savannah was exactly that.

Residents were here, sure, but there were more tourists and transients than those who hung around.

Was Lars a transient?

"Hello?" Lars waved a hand in front of Abilene.

His hand went far enough out that rain drops fell on it. He didn't seem to care. The rain had lessened and would soon be over but they still had to wait it out.

Lars pointed to a table nearby, where two people were almost getting up—or at least they looked like they were leaving. One of them opened an umbrella, and they were gone.

Abilene followed Lars to the table. As they were sitting down, she realized that the table was right outside a fudge shop. Her nose smelled freshly roasted pecan first. She tried to contain herself.

Lars lifted up a triangular cardboard from the center of their table. He read it aloud for Abilene. "For customer only."

Abilene told herself to resist, reminding her emotions that she had a few pounds to shed.

"Do you want anything?" Lars asked.

Abilene shook her head.

"Some fudge, perhaps?"

"Oh no. I'm on a diet."

Lars nodded. "A cup of hot chocolate, then?"

"No. Thank you. I'm fine. I brought water."

Abilene reached for her bag on the ground next to her chair.

When Lars disappeared into the shop, Abilene leaned against the back of the metal chair, her head resting on the exposed exterior brick wall of the fudge shop.

She closed her eyes to listen to the raindrops prattling on the canvas canopy above her.

"Sorry. Lost in thought. What was your question?"

"Bible study?" Lars raised an eyebrow. "Wednesday night?"

"Why?"

"Will you be there?"

Abilene didn't want to say either way, but then truth won out. "I usually am."

"Good. Ming asked me to go, but he has to work. I don't want to show up without really knowing anyone."

"You met Diego—Pastor Flores—and Nadine, Heidi, Ming. Don't be a stranger."

"Except you and I. We're still strangers." Lars stirred his hot chocolate.

Abilene found that amusing. It was almost summer, and here was Lars drinking hot chocolate in the middle of the morning. Sure, they'd been caught in the rain, and yes, it was still raining, but still...

"Look at us." Lars pointed to his own shirt and then Abilene's.

Us?

Abilene tried to focus on the faint blue and green paint traces she couldn't get totally off her arms.

There is no us.

A honk from the rainy street drew Abilene's attention. It was a car pushing through jaywalkers. Must be tourists driving the car. Everyone else would usually slow down to let the pedestrians cross. Beyond the street, the waterfront had a grayish-silvery tint to it all the way to the dark clouds in the sky. She could paint this scene sitting here, but it was too dreary for her. At this point in her life, she wanted something cheerful.

"Would that make a nice painting?" Lars asked.

No, he didn't read my mind. "Is that a random thought?"

"You're an artist. You're staring that way. Logic." Lars tried to frame the scene between his thumbs and index fingers. He moved his hands up and down. "I could paint the clouds. That would be easy. Just white and black paint, right?"

"There's a bit of dark brown up there."

"Where? I don't see any brown at all. I see all gray skies."

"Clouds are not all grayscale."

Lars peered through his make-believe lenses. "I see nothing."

"It's okay. Art is subjective. You draw and paint what you want." Abilene stared at her bottle of mineral water on the table. She wasn't reading the label. She wasn't sure what she was doing. She was getting more nervous by the minute.

Lars slapped his hands on his thighs and lifted his legs onto the third chair at the table. He crossed his arms behind his head.

"Ah, I could live here. This is the life. So laid back. No worries. No problems."

"Is that how you see life?" Abilene pulled out a sketchbook from her backpack on the ground. Her rolled-up, possibly destroyed painting of Hutchinson Island was leaning against the old nineteenth-century brick wall.

Mimicking her, Lars also produced a small sketch pad.

"You have a sketch pad too?" Abilene seemed amused.

"Yes, I do. I asked the art store for a starter kit, and it came with this and a pencil. I'm sorry to say that the pencil is overpriced."

"You could've asked me. I have spare pencils you can have for free."

"I didn't want to bother you."

"It's no bother." Abilene opened to an empty

page somewhere in the middle of her spiral-bound book. She began to draw.

"Say, may I have a look at your sketchbook?" Lars asked.

"You asked me about my age. Now you want to see my sketchbook."

"Well, if it's too personal…"

Personal?

Abilene thought for a moment, wondering if she'd drawn or written anything personal in the sketchbook. She didn't think so. "As soon as I finish this sketch."

"Yes, of course."

CHAPTER NINE

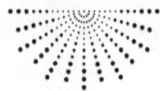

She took her time. He waited patiently.

Finally, not wanting to punish Lars for what he didn't do, Abilene handed over the sketchbook.

Lars lifted his own sketch pad in the air, as if to offer a swap. "Want to see mine?"

Abilene chuckled.

"What does that mean?" Lars asked.

"What does what mean?"

"The chuckle. Are you mocking me?"

"No, no." Abilene wasn't sure what to say. So why did she chuckle when he offered her his sketch pad? Well, for one thing, what could a novice artist possibly have in his sketch pad?

Novice?

She didn't know enough about Lars to determine if he was really a novice artist. "I'm sorry. It's just that you never said you were an artist or that you've drawn much in your life. I'm curious as to what you've put in that book."

"Well, here I am. An open book." Lars straightened up his shoulders.

Abilene laughed. "Nadine was right. You're a hoot."

"A hoot? Like an owl? Are you calling me a predator?"

That made Abilene laugh even more. She reached for his sketch pad. "All right. What's in here?"

Slowly, Abilene opened the sketch pad.

Calligraphy.

She was most surprised.

Poems.

Verses.

Snippets of writing. His thoughts?

"Wow. I'm impressed."

"Dear Abilene, you thought I had no useful skills."

Dear Abilene?

Abilene dared not look at him. She turned the pages. More ink. "These verses in calligraphy could be framed. Tell me more."

"My father left me a collection of calligraphy pens. My favorites are the quills, but they're too old to be used. I do write with reproductions sometimes. Glass quills if I feel like it."

"You should write more and see if Simon would take them for his gallery. He'd love this stuff."

"He would?" Lars brightened up.

"Sure. I'd buy them and hang them on my wall if I could—" As soon as the words came out of Abilene's mouth, she regretted them.

Can't get too close to this tourist. He's going home.

"If you could what?" Lars's eyes seemed to be searching.

"Nothing."

"I sense a hanging thought." Lars flipped through Abilene's sketchbook. "I love these scenes. Are they all local?"

Abilene nodded. "If I see something I like, I sketch it if I have time, or I take a photograph for later if I don't have time."

"Do you think anybody can do art? Draw like this, paint like you do?"

"Not exactly like I do. Perhaps even better. God has made each one of us unique, as you know. We all have different gifts and talents."

"You are amazingly talented, Abilene."

"I thank God every day for His grace to me, but to be sure, it's a lot of hard work."

Lars nodded. He was staring at a page. Abilene leaned over the table to see what was there.

Oh.

She didn't remember that sketch being in there. She'd had that sketchbook for a few years now and couldn't possibly remember everything she threw in there on the run.

But there it was. The impetus for her *Lady and the Sea* series. The one that had brought Lars all the way across the Atlantic Ocean on his quest.

She said nothing. Waited.

"This is the woman in your painting. The composite that you said has no history, no background."

"Not everything in art has a history, Lars. Sometimes I paint things on a whim, like I told you."

"But this has depth." He lifted the pencil sketch. "Something in her eyes. She is saying something. What is she saying?"

Abilene wanted to jump out of her chair and run. Just run. Away. From. Lars.

"She's not saying anything."

"Sadness?" Lars pressed.

"She's not sad!"

"Then what's in her eyes?"

"It's a pencil sketch."

"Uh-huh."

"You read too much into things that aren't there."

Lars smiled. "I'll buy you a whole box of maple pecan fudge if you tell me what's in her eyes."

Nadine! I'm going to kill her.

"No?" Lars smiled again. "How about I give a sizable donation to our church?"

"*Our* church? Your membership is still pending. Besides, you can't mess with God like that."

"Sorry. You're right. I'll give anyway. No strings attached."

"That's between you and God."

"And between you and me, how about all-you-can-eat maple pecan fudge?"

Abilene reached for her sketchbook in Lars's hands. He pulled it away and held it to his chest.

"May I have it back, please?" Abilene asked.

"One minute." He flipped to the next page. And the next. He lifted it for Abilene to see. "Nice house."

It was a sketch of that southern plantation-style beach house with the wraparound porch on both floors.

"Is this on Tybee Island?" Lars asked.

Abilene wondered how much to tell him. "I sketch what's in front of me."

"And you happened to walk past this house?"

"Something like that."

"What caught your eye?"

"The upstairs balcony. A place to paint all day out of the rain."

"Rain like this. Happens a lot in Savannah, I guess?"

"We're in the South. Rain comes with the territory. In fact, I have paintings of rain."

"But there was something about that house." Slowly, Lars slid the book across the table.

When Abilene reached for it, her fingers touched his. He locked his fingers into hers, his caked with dried green paint smeared on them, and hers streaked with a bit of oily tones here and there.

Their hands rested comfortably on top of her sketchbook.

His fingers were warm. Too warm.

"What's happening?" Abilene asked quietly.

"I'm not sure." Lars retracted his hand.

"You're here in town, trying to meet the nonexistent woman in my painting," Abilene reminded him.

"Exactly. I'm not after you."

"Right." At least they agreed on something, though Abilene wasn't sure she wanted to hear it come out of his mouth.

I'm not interested.

Still, it was good to clear the air. "To God be true, remember?"

Lars nodded. "Can't fall in love with an illusion."

"Right."

"But that woman in the painting is you, isn't she?"

Abilene raised her eyebrows. "Doesn't look like me, does she?"

"She's who you want to be."

"What are you now? A painting whisperer?"

That shut him up. Then: "There's a wall between us."

"You could say that. Like the fourth wall. I'm the artist. You're the art collector. We don't need to interact."

"Oh, that kind of wall."

"We hardly know each other, Lars." Abilene looked at the street, up to the sky, anywhere but across the table at Lars.

The rain was subsiding. People were returning to the waterfront. Good.

Abilene prayed to God that the sky would clear up some more. If her outdoor art classes were canceled, she didn't get paid.

Speaking of which...

She glanced at her watch. "I'd better go. I have stuff going on all day long."

"Like what?" Lars put up his palms. "Sorry. None of my business."

"Thank you for helping me with my easel."

"Sorry your painting is ruined."

"I don't know yet. I might be able to repair it." Abilene pointed to his shirt. "Hope you can get that lime-green paint removed."

"It's okay. It's just a shirt. I'll get another one if I have to. May I help you to your car?"

"Thanks, but no need. I'm not going to my car directly. I have to get to work and it's just several blocks down."

"You work?"

Abilene laughed.

"I thought you painted all day long."

"Painting is work!"

"Yes, yes. Sorry, I didn't meant to imply..."

"I'd rather be painting all day long, as a matter of fact, but I don't get to always do that, you know." Abilene checked her unfinished painting. It was still wet and damaged. Oh well. "I have to work to pay the rent and buy cat food."

"You have a cat?"

"Yes. Bradley is three." She swiped her iPhone and handed it to Lars.

"Oh, a ginger cat."

"American shorthair."

"Cute. Love his stripes."

"I do too." She took her iPhone back. "But I

must say his tail sometimes smears my paintings, usually just before the paint had a chance to dry."

"That's funny." Lars picked up his backpack.

Abilene wanted to ask him what he was doing the rest of the day, but then it would open doors she shouldn't open. Something about their locking fingers earlier told her that she'd better withdraw. She didn't feel safe opening her heart to someone just passing through at this time in her life.

Her life was going well. She painted whenever she wanted. Those teaching jobs at art studios made up for the balance of her income. She could afford her apartment. She'd paid off her little Honda.

She was happy alone. No need to complicate it with relationships that didn't last. She didn't need another travel mug to collect.

Best to remain single for a while until God brought her the right man she could share her life with. God had always provided for her.

To God be true, right?

CHAPTER TEN

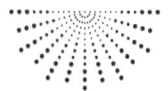

$\mathcal{I}$n spite of the rain earlier that morning, Fort Pulaski didn't have a shortage of visitors when Abilene walked into the fort from the wood bridge across the moat. The grass felt wet under her sandals.

In the middle of the fort, the Civil War cannon demonstration was underway.

A few of her students had arrived ahead of her, snapping shots of the fort and of the cannon demonstration. She smiled. They did that every Monday afternoon, taking pictures of the same arches and fortifications.

Abilene stood to one side, checking her emails on her iPhone. She had at least fifteen minutes to wait for the demonstration to be over, and that much time for the rest of her students to arrive. Some had been tardy stragglers, and Abilene did try to encourage everyone to be on time.

Most of her students were retirees looking for a new hobby, though a few of them had previous art training. Still, when they paid Simon's Gallery for the ten-week impressionistic painting class, her job was to teach them from square one, from perspective and sketching all the way to the finished painting of sections of the fort. Delays and absences only meant the students had catching up to do.

She had twelve students this time, and while she could take twenty, she was thankful for any number above ten. The pay was not great, and she had to teach five different art classes a week and supplement that with the sales of her paintings, but she made enough to get by.

Living alone had its perks. She only needed to shop for food for one person. Her small apartment didn't cost much to heat, and she could get by with very little. She found her clothes at consignment stores, and only splurged three years ago on one pair of those chunky-heeled pumps, which she'd been wearing to church on Sundays and to weddings. Those shoes had been the most expensive item she had personally bought. The rest of the time, her shoes came from Walmart.

No worries, really. She had no debt and no issues.

Yeah. No issues.

If Grandma Dupree found out how Abilene was saving money, she'd fly out here on her Gulfstream G650ER to straighten her out.

Never mind if Abilene wanted to see if she could make a living on her own without dipping into her trust fund—

"Hey, Miss Abilene!"

Abilene recognized that voice without even looking up. "Hey, Mr. Jacobs!"

Hiram Jacobs, a spritely retired pastor, spent his summer at the Savannah Senior Resort, a high-end senior community on Tybee Island, where the residents were pampered and doted on. Every now and then the resort would do on-site art classes, but those who were able to get around attended outdoor classes at various locations.

"Where's Ella?" Abilene asked.

Ella Brooks and Hiram Jacobs. What a pair. She wouldn't see them when summer was over, as they'd move back to their other senior living community on St. Simon's Island. Ella still had family on St. Simon's and Sea Island, and she wanted to spend Thanksgiving and Christmas with them.

"She's not feeling well today." Hiram shook his head.

"Sorry to hear that. I'll pray for her."

"Thank you. I always like a young lady who

prays. I should introduce you to my great-grandson. He's a pastor in Jacksonville, and he likes people who pray."

Uh-huh. His young *unmarried* twenty-seven-year-old great-grandson fresh out of seminary. She knew all about him because Hiram had been generous with the information.

"Well, tell Ella we miss her in class." Abilene said no more. She glanced at her iPhone. "Five more minutes. I'd better get to our classroom."

"Like some help with the chairs?" Hiram asked.

"Sure." Abilene led the way. All they would do was put out the folding chairs for the students who couldn't do it themselves.

"I'll help too."

At the sound of that voice, Abilene stopped in her tracks and spun around. Speechless.

"Nice to see you too, Abilene." Lars trotted toward them.

Hiram's eyes inspected Lars from head to toe. He stretched out his hand. "Hiram Jacobs. And you are?"

"Lars Cargill, sir. Nice to meet you."

"British?"

Lars nodded. "In town for the summer."

"Just the summer?" Hiram eyed him suspiciously.

"Yes, sir."

"Taking an art class with Miss Dupree here?"

"Yes, sir."

"No, sir." Abilene folded her arms.

"Check your email from Simon, Abilene." Lars turned those light-brown eyes on her. "Last minute addition."

Abilene checked her iPhone. Sure enough. She hadn't reached the latest email on her list, because she had started with the oldest email and worked her way up, but Hiram had interrupted her.

There it was. An *oh by the way* from Simon. Nice to have thirteen students in the class, but why did it have to be Lars?

"You know this is the third day of a ten-lesson class, right?" Abilene asked. "We've gone through the intro on perspectives and pencil sketches. Today we paint."

"No worries. I'm a fast learner. I'll catch up in no time."

"Okay. Welcome to the class, then."

"Thank you, I think."

Abilene led them to the red brick arches, where a few stacks of folding chairs were waiting for them. There were fifteen chairs there, more than enough.

From this spot, her students could see the entire parade ground and the distant arched doors, brick fortifications, and cannons on top of the walls, with tourists and their cameras under a clearing sky of blue streaked with white. All the while, they'd be shaded from the hot afternoon sun.

By the time everyone arrived and set up their chairs in their favorite spots, it was twenty minutes into the two-hour class, and at least two people had to go to the restroom.

Abilene was quite pleased to see Lars being such a helpful assistant to her, moving chairs for the seniors, setting up their easels, and carrying water buckets for them to clean their brushes. He was polite, and at least a few of the elderly ladies asked him if he was married.

"Not ever?" Squeals of delight reached an amused Abilene. They were followed by incessant chatter peppered with mentions of female names.

Lars looked embarrassed.

It was outside the scope of the class for Abilene to rescue a dude in distress. He could probably handle it himself.

She waited a bit.

Nope. Doesn't sound like it.

Sigh.

Abilene stepped in. "Ladies and gentlemen, we're about to start our painting session today. Mr. Cargill, will you please take your seat?"

Lars flashed his dimples as he passed by her to get to his chair. He mouthed a quick *Thank you.*

After briefly reviewing what they had covered in the last two lessons, Abilene let them loose.

She had her own canvas set up too, though she didn't plan on doing anything complicated. This was not a paint-by-numbers class, and she didn't have to finish her own painting, though she always did complete what she started. It had been ingrained in her even as a little child.

Never waste an effort.

She wanted to paint the skies above the parapet.

"Well, if they'd destroyed this fort in 1862, we wouldn't have anything to paint today," Hiram said loudly enough for everyone to hear.

He was sitting next to Abilene. She was about to ignore him, when he suddenly stood up.

Abilene wondered what Hiram was up to.

"Pop quiz, everyone!" Hiram declared. "Who was this fort named after?"

"What's the prize?" someone asked.

"I'll give you one of my brushes."

"Is it new?"

"Yes, ma'am. Brand new." Hiram waved a few brushes about. They still had price tags on them. "So. Does anyone know the answer?"

"Casimir Pulaski," Lars said before anyone else could raise their hands.

Abilene turned to find Lars sitting in the corner, facing a brick wall.

What's going on?

"You have to raise your hand and let me call you by name before you can answer the question," Hiram chided.

"Let the young and handsome and unmarried man win!" someone snapped at Hiram.

Hiram raised his arms to calm them down. "All right. We have a winner!"

He clapped. "A Revolutionary War hero, he was. Good for you, Lawrence."

"Lars," Lars corrected.

"Come get your brush anytime, Lawton."

"It's all right. I have plenty of brushes. Thanks, anyway." Lars continued painting, sitting in that corner.

Why is he sitting in a corner?

Abilene wanted to know, but she didn't want to make a scene. She'd get to him soon enough.

Ten minutes later, while her sky was drying, she made her rounds. Some of her students needed more assistance and guidance than others, but she assured them that there was no one way or wrong way to do Impressionism, even if they just copied what she had been painting. Details were sketchy at best, and it was up to the artist to convey the meaning of the painting.

She reached Lars in the corner soon enough. "So, facing the wall?"

"I'm painting historical bricks." Lars was deep in concentration.

On his canvas was a circle. Again. He was painting bricks in that circle.

"Do you ever draw outside the circle?" Abilene asked.

"Sometimes."

"What are you going to do about all that blank space around the circle of bricks?"

"Arches maybe."

"So you'll have to sit back several feet to change your focus."

"Maybe."

"Do you have questions for me?" Abilene asked, about to move on to the next student.

"Have dinner with me?"

Abilene was taken by surprise. "I meant about art. Impressionism. Your painting. This class."

"Nope. I might have some questions next week, but not today."

"Fine. Nice bricks, by the way." Abilene leaned toward the painting. "A bit too much detail for Impressionism, don't you think?"

"Is it?" Lars turned toward her. He was very close. Less than a foot away.

She could smell light aftershave and see small spots of reddish paint on his chin. She didn't have the heart to tell him.

Well, all right.

She pointed to her own chin. "Paint right here."

"Oh." He wiped it off. Now paint was on the back of his hand. And still on his chin.

Abilene took a clean rag from her apron pocket, dipped it in a bit of water, and wiped the paint off his chin. "There."

Lars didn't move.

Abilene ran her fingers through his paint brushes. She picked up a filbert brush with its round top. "Maybe instead of that script brush, you could try this."

"Okay." He took the brush from her, deliberately avoiding touching her hand.

"Miss Dupree!" a deep male voice called out from the other side of the outdoor classroom.

"Yes, sir?"

"I need some brush help too," he said.

Lars tried not to laugh. Abilene's eyes met his. He winked just slightly.

Abilene almost tripped on the flat cement floor as she walked away.

CHAPTER ELEVEN

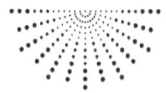

*A*bilene was painting the last bits of the morning sunrise into her beach scene against a backdrop of ocean waves and sea birds, when he came strolling across the shoreline into her line of sight, interrupting her view. Again.

She hadn't expected to see him.

Sigh.

She waited for him to come closer to her easel before she lobbed a brush at him.

But no, she held on to her expensive brush. "Are you stalking me?"

"In a bad mood today?" Lars asked. "Do you own this beach?"

"How did you know where to find me?"

"I looked for you at the river. You weren't there."

"And you called Nadine."

"And I called Nadine."

Abilene wondered, then decided to ask. "How did you get her number?"

"She has a website. Saylor Virtual Services."

"That's her. She told you I was here?"

Lars nodded.

"I'm going to kill her."

"Don't. She's already mad at me because I woke her up. I didn't know she wasn't up."

"She's a virtual assistant, as you know."

"Yeah, but still? It's daytime."

It was then that Abilene realized she and Lars were both early risers. What did that mean, exactly? She had no idea. But back to Nadine.

"She has clients overseas," Abilene explained. "The time differences sometimes mess her up."

"Well, what's done is done. She's upset with me. You're unhappy with me. I can't please anyone. I'm doomed."

"Silly pickle." Abilene resisted a smile.

"Just so you know this is your fault, I had to drink both cups of coffee because they'd get cold before I found you."

"Not my problem. I'm not sorry."

"You should be. I'm all jittery and need to run laps to work off all that caffeine."

"So go run. Run away. Far, far away."

"Yep. You're in a bad mood." Lars unzipped his easel bag.

"Could you please find your own spot?" Abilene pointed with her brush somewhere down the beach.

"Over there, you mean?"

"Out of earshot and out of sight, if possible."

"Do you hate me that much?" Lars hugged his bag.

"I don't hate you, Lars. I just need space. I need to get this painting done, or I won't get paid."

"I understand."

"Good."

"You like being alone." When Abilene said nothing, Lars went on. "You don't want to see where you and I might go because you think I'm leaving. We have some sort of feelings for each other, but we both fear our friendship might be a dead end."

"We're not friends. You're just visiting."

"Ah, therein is our problem."

Abilene kept on painting.

"What are you painting?" When she didn't respond, Lars came over. "Sunrise. Is this a part of the *Lady and the Sea* series?"

Abilene didn't reply.

"What about Hutchinson Island?"

Abilene washed a brush. "I work on multiple

paintings at the same time. I'll get back to the island soon."

"When?"

"I don't know. Really."

"Okay." Lars backed away. Ten or eleven feet away. That was as far as he went.

Abilene painted sand. Layers and layers of sand.

Minutes went by with silence between the two.

Abilene was enjoying the quiet in spite of Lars's presence. Above her, gulls and a couple of brown pelicans flew by. She painted the pelicans into her painting. She had a friend who ran a wildlife rehabilitation center. Someday she'd go there and paint more birds. For now, that pair of pelicans would have to do.

While she waited for the paint to dry, she texted Nadine to tell her to stop giving Lars information about her whereabouts. Nadine texted back *okay* and they made arrangements to meet for lunch at Piper's.

"Abilene?" Lars called her name.

She ignored him.

"Abilene?"

"Yes?" Abilene put away her iPhone.

"Do you have any viridian or brown ochre?"

What was she supposed to do? If she said no, it would be a lie. She was often overprepared and had all the tubes of paint she needed.

"No?" Lars asked. "You're a stingy person, Abilene Dupree. You can't even spare a dab of paint. How much does it cost? A penny? Two?"

He's piling on guilt. "All right. It's watercolor paint."

"I'm doing watercolor." Lars came over with a brush and his palette. She squirted the paint on his palette. After he had walked back to his easel, Abilene took a brush, went over to somewhere between her easel and his, and drew a line in the sand with her brush handle.

"If you cross this line, there's a penalty."

"Ooh. What is it?" Lars laughed.

Abilene rolled her eyes.

He literally walked toward her and stepped on the line.

"Stay on your side, Lars."

"What's the penalty?" Lars was inching closer, close enough for Abilene to reach him.

So she did.

She flipped her brush over and dabbed his shirt. His white shirt. Why did he wear such light-colored shirts?

Lars lifted his shirt with his fingers. "You call this art? Let me show you art."

His brush was quicker than Abilene could move aside. He dotted the front of her shirt with viridian.

"Unbelievable!" She tried to get away, but he

was fast. She felt brushstrokes across the back of her shirt. *Aarrgh!*

She ran toward her easel, found the biggest brush she had, and swiped up multicolored paint. He was in for it. She turned around to find him about to attack her with his brush. She moved faster than he did, painted his shirt, and then leapt away, laughing as she went.

He was furious and chased after her down the beach with his brush and arm outstretched.

A woman walking her dog stopped. "Teens! Grow up or get a room!"

"We're just reliving the childhood we never had!" Lars shouted as he chased a giggling Abilene down to the crashing waves.

Abilene lost her footing in the shifting sand, and she went splashing into the water. She emerged wet and embarrassed, her old brush floating away. "Oh no!"

In a valiant effort, if only to show off, Lars dove after the drifting brush. His long arms found purchase, and he grabbed the brush like a piece of treasure.

"My hero," Abilene spluttered.

"Am I?" Lars was dripping wet, his eyes sparkling under his stringy hair.

"Just joking."

"Are we?"

Abilene tried to take the brush back from him. He didn't release it. He pulled her hand to his chest, leaned down toward her wet face, and hesitated for a second before finding her lips.

CHAPTER TWELVE

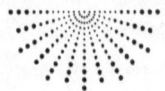

"*I* know! It's a bad idea." Abilene was drying her hair with a towel as she spoke into the speakers on her iPhone. "I don't even know this guy."

"Google is your friend. Look him up, girl." Nadine seemed to be eating something on the other end of the phone. Something crunchy.

"Isn't that an invasion of privacy?" Abilene wrapped the towel around her head. She plopped down onto her couch. Bradley the cat jumped up and sat on her tummy.

"Don't think he hasn't googled you already."

"I don't know, Nadine. I feel like we just met."

"You did just meet. A week ago, right?"

"Maybe almost two weeks."

"Right. We don't know anything about this guy."

"You're complicit in this, Nadine."

"What do you mean by that?" Nadine raised her voice.

"You told him where I was."

"I was barely awake. In fact, I don't recall much of the conversation." Crunch, crunch.

"But you did talk to Lars?"

"I might have."

Guilty!

"Say, have you thought of asking Ming to look into him?" Nadine asked.

"I can't afford Ming. You know that." Abilene looked out the open window.

Lots of sun out there. Perfect day to be outdoors. She had to be at Forsyth Park by three o'clock this afternoon for her class. She was teaching some teenagers to draw the fountain.

"I'll find out something and give you a report by next week. Maybe we could have lunch. Monday okay?"

Even if they didn't have boyfriends, Abilene and Nadine had each other. They had cried together over lost boyfriends and fiancés. Inevitably, everything could be solved by food. Usually lunch.

"Monday? It'll have to be short. I have to teach an art class at Fort Pulaski, remember?"

"Right. We'll go to Piper's. They're fast. Meanwhile, no more kissing. He might be carrying some sort of disease."

"Nadine!"

"I have to run. Have some work to do after lunch."

"Make sure you eat something healthier than chips for lunch."

"What's wrong with chips? They have veggies in them."

"Right." Abilene stroked her cat. After she hung up, she went to her laptop. Should she do this?

Well, it's public information.

"Let's do it." She sat down.

Bradley jumped up on the table and sat on her laptop.

"Bradley, no." Abilene picked him up and put him on the floor before she went online. After some keystrokes, she found Lars and his family.

Wow. Cargill Internet Communications.

No wonder he didn't have to work.

For sure she couldn't let this friendship or whatever continue. He might think that she only wanted to be with him because she knew he was from an affluent family and living off a trust fund. Truth was, that sort of thing had not crossed her mind. Then again, he couldn't tell, could he?

If Lars searched for Abilene online, he would

never find out about her background or her own trust fund from the Dupree hot sauce empire. She was living frugally like her parents had taught her, watching every penny, earning an income like most people do, driving an old used car, living in a small apartment, but it didn't mean she was impoverished.

There were many people poorer than she was in refugee camps, villages, and cities all over the world. There were many kids who had no money to go to college. Some of them were good Christian kids who wanted to go to seminary. She felt good helping them. Feed the world, feed the soul. But he didn't need to know that.

Would his view of her change if he learned that she probably could match his trust fund?

Seriously, did it all matter in the end?

Why couldn't two people enjoy each other without all their baggage?

CHAPTER THIRTEEN

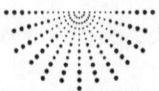

"Y̶ou can hardly see the lady." Lars pointed to the smudge of red paint at the edge of the sand where the surf came in on Abilene's painting. He wondered why Abilene didn't make the person bigger. Put her in the foreground.

"Are you an art critic now?" Abilene dabbed more paint.

"I'm a collector, remember?" Lars rubbed his chin with his fingers. "So why is there such a big space in the foreground?"

"Wait and see."

"Wait and see? Does this mean you're not telling me to go away today?" He showed his most affable smile to get into Abilene's good graces.

She seemed a bit withdrawn. Did she regret his

kissing her two days before? To be fair, she hadn't pulled away. She seemed to enjoy it.

Maybe it was his imagination, but if she was upset about it, she hadn't shown it at last night's Bible study at Ming's house. Well, she hadn't talked to him much. They had sat across from each other, but her eyes were on her Bible almost the entire Bible study, which only lasted an hour.

This morning was the first time they could be together. Alone, Abilene seemed to be able to speak freely to him.

Perhaps she was a bit shy in a crowd, like at church last Sunday. She had seemed nervous to be near him. But when they were together, just the two of them, whether at the riverfront or oceanfront here, she seemed more conversational.

Most of the time.

"I know so little about you, Abilene."

"Don't you have a painting to finish?" she asked.

"Already done."

"Really?"

"I'll show you." Lars went back to his easel ten feet away, crossing and recrossing the line in the sand that he had redrawn for Abilene's sake.

He was proud of his little painting. He had added a little sandpiper against a backdrop of sand, surf, sea, and sky. Up in the clouds, he had added more colors to his flying pelican.

Abilene studied the artwork.

"Like it?" Lars waited for the verdict.

"It's a good start."

"Meaning what? It's amateurish?" Lars tried to hide his disappointment.

"No. Colorful." Abilene pointed to the top right-hand corner of the painting. "What's that?"

"A pelican. Can't you tell?"

"It's a smudge."

"A smudge? Is that an insult?"

"I didn't realize you're sensitive."

"I am not."

"That proves it. Defensive, aren't you?"

"Me? Not a bit. Say what you will, but I like what I painted."

"Like I said, it's colorful. You should sign it."

"I will. Do you have a brush I can borrow for that?" Lars started digging through Abilene's tray of brushes.

"Sure. Pick a fine one. And practice signing on a test canvas first."

"Good idea. Do you have a spare canvas?"

Abilene rolled her eyes. She dug into her backpack and handed Lars a thick piece of heavy paper.

"Thank you. I owe you."

"No, you don't." Abilene stared at her painting as if she saw something there.

Lars wanted more. "How about dinner tonight?"

"No."

"Come on. We'll pay our own way. It won't be a date." Lars didn't want to sound like he was pleading. But, yeah, he was. "We're just fellow artists. Two painters sharing a meal."

"If you put it that way."

"I'll pick you up?" He liked his rental car, though he had to drive on the other side of the road.

Usually, when he traveled to foreign countries, he would use taxies and drivers. He felt freer driving himself to places this time. So far, Tybee Island was the farthest he had driven from the riverfront hotel he was staying in.

"No need," Abilene said. "Tell me where, and we'll meet there."

"What would you like to eat? Maybe you can recommend a restaurant." He waited for Abilene to come up with a name. She named a place that he hadn't heard of. It was on River Street.

"It's probably not too busy tonight, considering it's Thursday," Abilene explained.

"I'll go with that since you know the place."

"I don't go there all the time. The last time I went it was with—uh, never mind."

"I don't need to know." Lars smiled.

Abilene nodded. "Really, it was over a long time ago. College sweethearts and all that."

"Right. I used to date this girl at university too. I

was in love with her. I mean, I was ready to marry her."

"Sounds serious."

"Turned out she was dating my cousin at the same time. I mean, I can't imagine sleeping with two —never mind."

Abilene's face turned pink. Deep pink. Beet red now.

"I'm sorry, Abilene." Somehow Lars felt he had to explain. "It was five or six years ago. I was a prodigal son. I stopped attending church, and I broke Mother's heart. I returned to God two years before Mother passed away."

"Glad she could see you come back to God."

"I know." Lars's voice started to crack.

He cleared his throat. He never meant to say all these things to Abilene. They were just going out to dinner.

Then again, it was good for his conscience to be transparent to her. Straying from God hadn't been something he had done on purpose. It had begun as a slow drift in high school, his pride and rebellion pushing him away from God, followed by falling into Yona's company and that of her friends. He should never have dated someone who didn't have respect for his God, but he had let it happen. He had been weak and stupid.

"We all have our pasts," Abilene said.

"I have asked God to forgive me. And my mother did before she passed away."

"God's forgiveness is always complete."

"Yet there are always repercussions," Lars added. "Sowing and reaping."

Abilene nodded. "If you wanted corn and you planted peanuts, you can be forgiven, but you're still stuck reaping peanuts and no corn. Or vice versa."

"I know what you mean. The scars remain."

"God can heal you and give you a new start."

"Yes. Jesus can cleanse us from all sins." Lars swiped his iPhone. "My memory verse and I'm almost forgetting it."

He read 1 John 1:9 to Abilene.

If we confess our sins, He is faithful and just to forgive us our sins and to cleanse us from all unrighteousness.

"I like that verse."

"I do too."

"Well, I need to get back to this painting." Abilene picked up her palette. "Thanks for sharing, Lars."

"Okay. I'll go back to my side of the fence now. Is dinner still on tonight?"

"Sure. Why not? We have to eat."

Lars smiled. For a moment there he was

concerned she would change her mind. He couldn't believe he had brought up his past with Yona. To be sure, he had been pure since they'd broken up. He'd been living the narrow life thereafter.

Yes, his life had drifted, but he had returned to God since he repented of his sins. His brother, Colm, could testify to that.

Was he drifting again?

Maybe a little bit. He had no real job to speak of, and wondered what to do with the rest of his life.

He could go home to England and work for Cargill Internet Communications and put his Yale MBA to good use, but since he had arrived in Savannah, he liked it here. He could always start a business and get a permit to stay in this country. For now,` he was on a tourist visa for the rest of the summer. After that, who knew?

More than likely, nothing would happen between him and Abilene, and he'd go home to London for the rest of his life, while she stayed here for hers.

Somewhere in his heart he hoped there was more to life than just passing through.

Lord Jesus, there is more, isn't there?

CHAPTER FOURTEEN

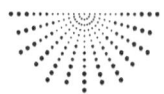

*R*iver Street on Thursday night was as busy as any other night except the first Friday night of every month with its fireworks over the river.

Abilene didn't know why she decided to wear her expensive pumps that had worn down over the last few years. She wished she had prettier shoes but she knew she wouldn't wear them often. Her matching deep-purple dress was secondhand, but no one needed to know that.

Oh yes, don't anybody tell Grandma Dupree or Mom where I shop.

She'd be summoned home to New Orleans to live in opulence, which wouldn't be her style.

Here she was in a cheap dress with fluffy sleeves and old pumps with scratches on the heels. No one could see those scratches, Abilene reminded herself, because it was at night. Wearing new shoes across those cobblestones would be silly.

Besides, she doubted Lars had noticed anything about her. Had he even noticed that she wore a bracelet tonight? It was from Grandma Dupree, and it was one of the Dupree family heirlooms.

"I enjoyed dinner tonight," Lars said as they stopped to watch a container ship slide by on the Savannah River. "Thank you for going with me."

"It was fun."

"Do you want any dessert?"

"I can't eat any more."

"Me neither."

"So why did you ask?"

"To prolong the evening. I'm afraid you'll want to leave."

Abilene reached for Lars's left arm and peered at his watch. Realizing what she was doing, she retracted her hand.

"Oh, sorry. I forget. My brother has a watch like that, and I often grab his arm and check the time myself."

"I remind you of your brother." Lars frowned.

"I don't mean that. I just wanted to know the time—never mind."

"And you didn't think to ask."

"Ask?"

"You can grab my hand anytime, but you could have asked for the time."

"Are you overreacting?"

"No. I'm just pointing out that you feel comfortable with me, Abilene."

"Maybe I do, but I don't want to be familiar with you."

"For the record, we kissed."

"Once."

"Doesn't that mean anything?" Lars looked hurt.

Abilene couldn't read it. "It was spontaneous. You rescued my paintbrush from the ocean."

"You called me your hero."

"I was only kidding."

"I didn't take it that way."

"You really should." Abilene kept walking.

Lars reached for her hand. She felt the gentle touch.

They walked together holding hands, silence between them, backdropped by the sounds of people chatting, street musicians playing soft pop music, ships sailing, vehicles going down the road, wheels on cobblestones.

Abilene drank in the night, the contrasting quiet of the stars and clouds above them, the canopy of the southern night.

The clouds parted, revealing the moon casting a grayish hue on them as they strolled by the river.

A wispy breeze sent a chill up Abilene's bare arms.

Lars seemed to notice. He slid his arm across her shoulders. He was warm to the touch.

He leaned down and kissed her cheek lightly.

"What was that for?" Abilene asked.

"Does a hero have to explain everything?"

"You saved an old paintbrush."

"A hero's a hero."

"We'll never live this down."

"We'll be telling our grandchildren the same story—sorry."

Grandchildren?

Abilene felt herself going rigid under Lars's arm.

"I said sorry," Lars added.

"No worries. Sometimes we say things we don't mean."

Lars nodded. But the expression on his face under the moon said he had meant it.

CHAPTER FIFTEEN

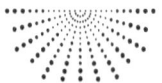

"We agreed you should stay away from him until I get you some news." Nadine shook her head as if Abilene's infraction would send her away for years. "Good thing it turned out he's legit. So now you can tell me all about your date night."

Abilene stretched on her favorite couch in her small living room. She stared at Nadine sitting with her legs folded underneath her on the armchair across the coffee table. Her college friend was wearing some seriously bright pink shorts and an equally fluorescent orange shirt.

"Where did you get that outfit?" Abilene waved a hand.

"Focus, Abilene. How was your date with Lars?"

"We ate. We walked. We went home separately. The end."

"Did you kiss again?"

"No. He gave me a friendly peck on the cheek."

"You're turning pink." Nadine leaned forward. "You like him, don't you?"

"Maybe a little. It can't last. He's leaving at the end of summer or sooner if his brother needs him at work."

"I doubt it." Nadine waved her Android phone about. "It says here that when their parents died, they left the two sons a fortune."

Abilene had read all that herself. "Did you google, or do you have anything more than public info?"

"Well, Ming did us a favor and dug around."

"I don't want to owe him anything."

"You don't owe him. You owe me. I'm cooking dinner next Tuesday night for him and Sabine."

"I didn't offer to cook for them."

"You can't. You burn everything."

"I do not." Abilene nearly sat up.

"You only make sandwiches. One wonders how you grew up."

"Mom cooked. We never starved."

Nadine threw up her arms. "Never mind. You still owe me."

Abilene laughed. "I'm always owing you,

Nadine. Stop helping me, and I won't be in your debt anymore."

"When I need some help, I'll call you."

"You're going to call? That'll be the day. We all know you're too independent. You don't need any help."

"Someday I might."

"But not today!" They said it together.

"Want to know more about Lars Tabansi Cargill?" Nadine settled back into the armchair. Without waiting for Abilene to reply, she went on. "Did you know Tabansi means endurance?"

"His mother was born in Botswana." Abilene picked up the can of mineral water from the coffee table beside the couch.

"He told you that?"

"How else would I know?"

"I thought maybe you googled ahead of me."

"You're competitive." It was all Abilene said. Sure, she had searched for his information, but on the surface. She didn't like to pry. Nadine, on the other hand, was the inquisitive one. Good or bad? She had no idea.

"His dad was one Rupert Cargill. Rupert's family was part Scottish, part Danish, and part Tswana in Botswana. By the way, Lars was named after his maternal great-grandfather from Copenhagen."

"Quite a multiethnic family," Abilene said. "Any French in there?"

"Not Creole like your family." Nadine hated to be interrupted, but Abilene had to know.

"Anyway, Rupert Cargill started Cargill Internet Communications back in the eighties. Around that time, he was on a business trip to Gaborone when he met a lady named Kayla Modipe, a family friend."

"Gaborone?"

"Capital city of Botswana. Next thing you know, Rupert and Kayla were married. Two beautiful boys were born, and they all lived happily ever after in a big house in London."

"How sweet."

"Well, until Rupert had a massive heart attack and died while the boys were still in high school."

"That's terribly sad."

"After secondary school—that's high school for us—Colm went to Oxford and Lars came here to the States. Yale."

"Yale. Interesting."

"MBA to boot. Kayla Modipe-Cargill took over the business after Rupert passed away. She died of cancer last year."

One year after Lars had returned to Christ. "Very sad indeed."

"The older brother, Colm, pretty much mentored your Lars."

"He's not *my* Lars." Abilene nearly spilled the mineral water over herself.

"If you kissed, something's going on. Your Lars."

Abilene was about to protest when Nadine held up a hand. "Nothing is ever just a kiss."

"Well, maybe there was a bit more. Maybe we want to know each other more."

"Honesty is good. Go on."

"But we're strangers. It can't last." Abilene rolled over on her back on the couch. Again, Bradley jumped on her tummy and settled down for a nap.

"You remember when I was dating Doyle, maybe a couple of years back?" Nadine asked.

"Yeah. You met him in the ice cream shop."

"Exactly. So it can happen, Abilene."

"Doyle didn't last."

"Nineteen months, Abilene. An eternity in my world."

"I want happily ever after. A lifetime of love."

"Only God's love lasts forever."

"Exactly. I want him to love me with God's love. Until death do us part." Abilene stroked Bradley's back. He purred. "If he can't give me God's love, then it's only human love, and it won't last."

CHAPTER SIXTEEN

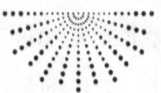

*W*ith the approval of her friends, Nadine and Ming, Abilene felt comfortable to keep going out with Lars. She hadn't broached the subject yet about the end of summer.

For three Sundays in a row, Lars appeared like clockwork at church. Each time, Abilene had refused his offer to pick her up. It would be a long way to her house from his hotel, which was across the street and down a few blocks from Riverside Chapel. He could walk to church. On the other hand, Abilene had to drive through at least five or six squares to get to church.

"We welcome our brother in Christ, Lars Cargill, to Riverside Chapel," Pastor Flores said to the applause of the congregation plus visitors.

Sitting at the back of the dining room, Abilene

surveyed the Sunday morning crowd. Attendance was down today, but summertime aside, Abilene thought that most people would consider a riverboat church a gimmick. She did agree with the other charter members that they should move to a church building soon, before the owner of the riverboat took it back.

One more year to double church membership. Or not.

Lars walked toward Abilene and sat down beside her.

"That was easy," he said.

"Now you'll be put to work," Abilene whispered.

"Doing what?"

"Whatever is needed."

"Great. Do they pay well?"

"Your reward is all in heaven."

"Where moth and rust don't destroy?" Lars grinned at her.

He seemed to know his Scripture. Good for him.

The congregation sang some more, and then Pastor Flores continued his sermon series on being true to God. Abilene was pleased to see that Lars was taking notes on his iPhone. She preferred a spiral-bound notepad. She jotted down the verses for later and took down some points of application.

Church was over too soon, and then there was the question about lunch.

"Don't say no," Lars began.

"No what?"

"You know. Look, I can pay for your lunch. Don't worry about it. I just want you to come. It's not the same without you."

"My cat's home alone all day."

"Your cat." Lars shook his head. "Bradley?"

"You remember my cat's name."

"Bradley's more important than I am."

"For the record, I've known him longer than I've known you. How long have I known you? A month? I've had Bradley for three years."

"Point taken. Okay. We'll pick up something, and we'll eat at your house with your cat."

Abilene was alarmed. "You can't come to my house."

"Why not?"

"I haven't vacuumed. Cat hair is everywhere."

"I don't care."

The crowd thinned. Nadine came over. "Don't care about what?"

"Cat hair," Lars said.

"We're fighting over Bradley?" Nadine asked.

"We're not fighting," Abilene explained. "I just need to go home."

Lars leaned toward Abilene. "You miss your cat."

"It's been four hours."

"You miss your cat."

"You're repeating yourself, Lars."

"But you don't miss me."

"I don't know." Abilene started walking away, keys jingling over her Bible and notebook. "I need to go. See you tomorrow at the fort."

Lars went after her. "Wait."

Abilene turned around.

"I'm sorry I invited myself to your house. I just wanted to have lunch with you."

"Don't worry about it." Abilene looked at Nadine, who was standing behind Lars. Waiting?

"If you don't have any plans, Nadine, would you like to have lunch at my house too?"

"Sure. Ming and Sabine are out of town. The Floreses have family in town. I don't have anyone but you guys."

Nadine was at it again. Probably her monthly cycle or something. It made her emotional like that.

"Splendid," Lars said. "Lunch is on me. What do you feel like eating?"

"We always get lunch from Piper's Place, though there are other options," Abilene suggested. "I like their quick organic meals."

"I like organics too." Lars turned to Nadine.

"What say you?"

"I'll eat anything." Nadine led the way. "I drove this morning, so I'll just see you there."

"I'll drive," Abilene suggested to Lars.

"You live a long way from here, you said. Maybe I should take my own car so you don't have to drop me off later."

"Sounds good." Abilene appreciated his care.

Somewhere in between those lines, she suspected he was giving her space. Her previous boyfriends hadn't understood her need to breathe and they had smothered her.

Lars was different.

And no, Lars was not her boyfriend. He was just passing through town and going home.

"Text me your address," Lars said.

Abilene did, though at the back of her mind she wondered about the wisdom of that. Oh well. They had all agreed to eat lunch at her house.

Lars's iPhone pinged. "Great. You go home and tidy up, if you must. But leave me the vacuuming."

"You want to vacuum my house?" Abilene chuckled.

"Are you insulting my lack of useful skills?" Lars held her hand as they went down the ramp toward the waterfront.

"Why, I wouldn't want to do that. Feel free to come over and vacuum my house."

CHAPTER SEVENTEEN

"*S*he gives away all her money to missions and charities," Nadine declared from one of two couches in Abilene's living room.

"Nadine, TMI." Abilene sat on one of two swivel stools at the kitchen peninsula.

She had freed up her favorite couch for Lars to sit on, but he had been standing by her paintings since lunch was over.

She didn't want him rummaging through her paintings and discovering the original *Lady and the Sea*, which she had tucked away into her coat closet before everyone else arrived.

"Not too much info." Nadine patted the throw pillow she was hugging. "He needs to know."

"I do?" Lars left the paintings alone—for which Abilene was grateful—and sat down on one end of her favorite couch. He motioned for her to share the couch with him, but she just smiled. What could she say?

"Yeah, I think so." Nadine rambled on. "Did you know her grandma started a hot sauce empire that has gone global?"

"Hot sauce?"

"Killer hot sauce."

"Killer? Is that what it's called?"

Abilene laughed. "Might as well be."

"What did they almost call it, Abilene?" Nadine turned her head toward Abilene.

"Sauce of Life," Abilene said. "Grandma Dupree said no. She said Grandpa wouldn't have approved it."

"Why?" Lars asked.

"Sounded too close to *source of life*. Grandpa didn't think that a simple, homemade hot sauce is worthy of that honor. The source of life is God and God alone." Abilene slid off her old stool and went to the refrigerator to get a can of mineral water.

"So they called it Hot Dupree," Nadine chipped in.

"Anyone want something to drink?" Abilene asked. "I have juice, milk, mineral water, soda... That's all I have."

"Nothing for me," Lars said. "I'm stuffed from

lunch. I'll be going back there tomorrow for the same couscous soup."

"They sometimes use Hot Dupree," Nadine offered.

Abilene wondered how to make Nadine shut up about her family. She had always been a private person, and here was Nadine spilling the beans or, should she say, hot sauce. Lars didn't seem like he wanted to know.

"So." Nadine sat up and faced Lars sitting across the coffee table.

What is she up to now?

Abilene's fingers shook a little as she drank her mineral water. She was still standing in the kitchen. The peninsula was no protection for her from her friend.

"Lars Tabansi Cargill," Nadine began.

Uh-oh.

Just then, Bradley jumped off the patio chair and strolled into the living room. He eyed Lars. He rubbed against Lars's dress pants. Lars reached down to stroke his fur.

Then Bradley did something Abilene hadn't expected. The cat leapt onto the couch and nuzzled Lars's arm. When Lars patted his head and spoke kindly to him, Bradley purred and settled down on the couch next to Lars.

My cat likes Lars.

Surprise, surprise.

Bradley hadn't liked almost all of Abilene's ex-boyfriends, least of all Winton Pace. He had told Abilene if she wanted to continue their relationship, either the cat had to leave or he had to go.

After much weeping and praying, Abilene had shown Winton the door.

Someone had to go.

"You know my full name." Lars leaned back and put a long arm on the back of the couch.

"It's on your business card," Nadine said.

"The one I gave to Abilene, not to you." His eyes were on Abilene.

"She wanted to see it." Abilene shrugged.

"Do you want to see my passport or driver's license too?" Lars asked.

"No need. Ming—" Nadine's palm went to her mouth.

"Ming, the PI?" Lars kept his eyes on Abilene. "You did a background check on me."

His voice was low. Calm and cool. Extremely collected.

"I didn't." Abilene raised both hands, nearly spilling her mineral water all over her blouse and skirt.

"Don't blame her. It was my idea," Nadine confessed. "I have to protect my friend. Besides, Ming owed me a favor."

"Nice to have friends like that, don't you think, Abilene?" Lars turned his attention to Nadine.

Abilene was relieved. Somewhat. She managed a grin. "She investigated all my ex-boyfriends."

"Sounds like my brother."

Nadine sat up. "Your brother? Is he married?"

"Nadine!" Abilene sighed.

Lars chuckled. "Colm is married to his work."

"Oh, that kind of monogamy."

Abilene couldn't believe what her friend said. She wanted to change the subject. Talk about the pretty May weather. Anything.

But Lars beat her to it with what seemed to be on his mind.

"What did you find out about me, Nadine?"

"Nothing much, Lars. Don't worry."

"What I thought. I have a boring life."

"You do—" Nadine nearly fell off the couch when the horrid ringtone sounded on her iPhone.

Abilene had told her to change it into something more mellifluous, but that wasn't Nadine. Nope. It had to be gongs and drums and something bizarre and off key from some no-name garage band.

"I have to take this call." Nadine went to the foyer and out the front door, leaving Abilene alone with Lars. Well, not exactly alone. Bradley the cat chaperoned, even if he was sleeping now, cuddled up on the couch next to Lars's thigh.

"Nice cat," Lars said.

"He seems to like you." Abilene chuckled. "He didn't like—uh."

"Your ex-boyfriends."

"Bradley is a good judge of character."

"Is he?" Lars kept stroking the cat's fur. Bradley didn't seem to mind.

Oh, but Abilene minded. Yes, she minded very much.

CHAPTER EIGHTEEN

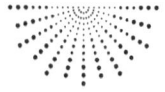

"*Y*our friend Nadine is interesting." Lars meant it.

He wondered why Abilene didn't join him on the couch. She appeared alone, aloof, apart, sitting there on that barstool, then pacing back and forth around the peninsula.

It seemed to him she'd been reticent.

She hadn't made eye contact since lunch. If she looked in his direction, it was to keep an eye on her cat sleeping peacefully next to Lars.

Surrounding them were noises from outside, chirps of birds on trees, the occasional sirens and revving of vehicles from the street, and the muted chatter of Nadine on the phone outside the front door that she must have left cracked.

"Are you concerned about what comes out of your friend's mouth next?" Lars pried.

"She means well." Abilene folded her arms.

Yep. That told him something too. She was putting a mental shield between herself and him.

"I'm sure she does." Lars didn't move, because he didn't want to wake the cat. He wanted to show Abilene that he got along with her precious pet.

"This is a cozy place." Change of subject.

"I've been here since my SCAD days."

Lars wanted to comment that the cost of this apartment was probably pretty low, but he thought better of it.

It was becoming apparent to him that Abilene could have had a nicer place, a better car, and so forth. But then, to each her own.

"Is this a rental?"

"Yes. Why?"

"I'm wondering why you haven't bought your own house."

"It's none of your business."

"You've been here awhile. Planning on moving away?"

"From Savannah? No. I like this place."

"Then what's stopping you from buying something permanent, settling down?"

"I don't know. Haven't found a place, maybe."

"How about that house in your sketchbook?"

Beside Lars, Bradley the cat didn't stir. Lars kicked off his shoes, lifted his long legs, and crossed his feet on the coffee table between the two mismatched couches.

"It's not for sale."

"If it were, you'd have bought it?"

Abilene hesitated. Lars counted the seconds or minutes that passed by.

"Yes. I probably would."

"Meanwhile, you stay in this little place with your cat and give the rest of your money away to charity."

"Not all of it. I do put something into retirement, in case..."

"In case you live alone all your life."

Abilene glanced in the direction of the front door, as if waiting for Nadine to come in and break up their conversation.

Was she uncomfortable because he was in her house?

Was he getting in her personal space?

They had kissed. What about that?

"I don't need much to live on," Abilene explained. "I'm single, the cat's single. We just need a roof over our head, food on the table, and a job. I have no debt, no worries. What more could I ask?"

"No worries?" Lars smiled. "We all have worries."

"Well, God did say not to worry or be anxious about anything."

"Philippians 4:6-7."

Be anxious for nothing, but in everything by prayer and supplication, with thanksgiving, let your requests be made known to God; and the peace of God, which surpasses all understanding, will guard your hearts and minds through Christ Jesus.

"You know your Scripture."

Lars nodded. "In the last couple of years I've gotten into the Word more and more to atone for—well, you know."

"We all have pasts."

"Mine might be more colorful than yours."

"Ha-ha. Sure. Ming and Nadine—bless their hearts—unearthed nothing but blah in your life."

"Blah? Is that what they said?"

"Oh, sorry. No. I paraphrased them. I didn't mean..."

"Never mind, Abilene. God has been good to me. He took me back and straightened me up."

"God is always good."

It sounded like the front door opened. Nadine hurried to pick up her purse. "I have to run. My new client wants to meet and talk in person. Thanks for lunch, Lars. See you two tonight at church. Don't do anything I wouldn't do."

"Nadine!" Abilene's face turned a bright pink.

Lars got up gently so that he did not wake the cat. "Where's your vacuum? I'd better get started if we don't want to miss evening church."

"Bradley is sleeping. I'll vacuum later."

"I gave you my word."

"I'm canceling our agreement. Really. Go home."

"Are you trying to get rid of me?" Lars checked the coat closet.

No vacuum in there, but—

"What's that?" He spotted something leaning against the back wall of the closet. As he was pushing aside coats, he spotted a woman's wool coat. Valentino.

Valentino?

There was so much more to Abilene he didn't know. He pushed that thought aside and was about to reach for the frame when a hand grabbed his arm.

"The vacuum is not in here, Lars."

Her touch went through his silk oxford shirt. It was gentle but *don't go there* firm.

He backed away from the closet. He thought he saw a corner of a painting, but if Abilene had a problem with it, there was nothing more he could do.

This was her house.

Her domain.

"I'm sorry," he said instead.

"No problem." She shut the closet door. "Seriously, there is no need for you to buy me lunch and vacuum my house."

"Too much, too soon?"

"No. I mean, yes. Well, it's awkward, if you know what I mean."

"I don't know what you mean." Lars's fingers brushed past some curls over her ear. "You have curly hair. I like it."

"I got it from Grandma Dupree. Lots of my family members have straight hair." Abilene backed away. "I inherited a lot of traits from her except business sense."

"You're an artist."

"Doesn't mean I can't do business, but what I'm saying is that I'd rather paint all day."

"Sounds like a dream job." Lars looked down to find Bradley rubbing against his dress pants. "Hey there, little fellow. Thought you were napping."

When he straightened up, Abilene was staring at him. "What, Abilene? Something wrong?"

"Nothing's wrong. Watch out for his claws. They can leave scars."

Lars picked up Bradley. "Did you hear that, Bradley?"

The cat purred.

Still carrying Bradley, Lars followed Abilene to her laundry closet, where, tucked in a corner, was an old vacuum cleaner. He wondered how well it worked, if it worked at all.

Abilene uncoiled the cord, parts of which had duct tape on it.

For some reason Lars wanted to get her a new vacuum cleaner.

"Do you know how to use this?" Abilene asked as she plugged the vacuum into a nearby wall socket.

"Push a button and it runs?"

"I wish." She showed him where the button was and how to move the cleaner around. "Really, Lars, this is weird."

"What's weird?"

"Vacuuming on your first day at my house."

"First day?" Lars studied her. "You mean I get to come back?"

"Only if Bradley approves." Abilene took the cat from Lars.

"I didn't get scratched." Lars smiled.

"Good. I don't want to get sued."

"He likes me." Lars stroked Bradley's head. He purred again.

"Seems like it."

"Is that good?"

"That's very good, Lars. Win—uh, my ex-boyfriend hated cats. He wanted me to get rid of Bradley."

"What a shame. He looks like a good cat."

"I rescued him when he was a kitten. No way was I going to give him away."

"So you got rid of your ex instead."

Abilene nodded. "Someone had to go."

The thought was not lost on Lars.

CHAPTER NINETEEN

*L*ars hadn't been able to talk with Abilene since the Sunday night service. She had been busy working at Simon's Gallery, filling in for someone, then running to teach classes here and there.

At the Fort Pulaski art class on Monday afternoon, she had been busy too, and he had left her alone so she could offer personal assistance to almost every art student in her packed class.

It was Thursday now, and he knew that if he came out here early enough, he'd find Abilene.

And there she was.

June was turning warm, but it was early in the month. He wasn't sure if he liked the humidity, but he'd find out soon enough when July and August came around.

August? Did he intend to stay that far into the summer in the States?

He liked the place, liked the people, and loved—

Loved?

He caught himself. He refocused his thoughts on Abilene's painting. It wasn't the one she had started.

"What happened to the other painting?" Lars asked, finger on his shaved chin, as he stood there in the morning breeze.

"You mean the painting with the smudge that you complained about?" Abilene stood on the other side of her folding chair to finish her coffee.

Lars wondered if the chair between them meant something. Another barrier?

"Thanks for the coffee," Abilene said. "You know you don't have to. I don't want to put you out."

"It's nothing."

"Ten dollars a day is nothing to you?"

"Not in the company of a beautiful lady."

"Are you bribing me with coffee?" Abilene put her fists on her waist.

"I didn't mean it that way."

"Yeah. I know." Abilene sat down in front of her blank canvas.

"About the other painting?" Lars asked again.

"I'm going to paint the foreground soon. I just don't have any idea what I want to put there yet."

"Is this part of the *Lady and the Sea* series?"

"Yes. But the lady is the smudge, remember?"

"Ah. So you need to paint over it."

"I need to fix it somehow."

Lars backed away. He knew she wanted her space. "I'll let you work."

"Okay. You have everything you need? Paint, brushes?"

"Yes. I'm prepared today."

"Good for you."

He went to his own easel. He drew another circle and painted it bright yellow. Done.

He wondered how much more art he needed to learn to spend more than five minutes on his canvas. He glanced over at Abilene. She was still staring at the blank canvas. No paintbrush or palette in her hands.

"You okay?" he hollered.

"Yeah."

"I finished my painting."

"Yeah?"

He lifted it toward her so she could see it.

"It's a yellow circle. What else are you adding to it?"

"I don't know. I need inspiration."

"Funny. So do I." Abilene sighed.

"Let's take a walk. Find some ideas."

"Okay." Abilene got off her chair. She took the canvas off the easel and folded it up.

"What are you doing?"

"If we get inspired while walking, I don't want to have to come back here to get my canvas."

"Good thinking." He also packed up his stuff. He put the yellow canvas on the sand. It was drying in the warming sun. When he picked it up again to follow Abilene down to the shoreline, he noticed that there was sand on his canvas, stuck to the yellow paint.

He pointed to the annoyance.

"Use a paper towel and gently scrape it off," Abilene said. "You might need to repaint a bit."

He decided to do it later. They walked at the foamy edge. The ocean came up to their ankles. Abilene's flip-flops were stashed into the mesh pocket of her backpack. She was holding the folding chair under an arm.

"Let me have that." Lars took the chair away from Abilene before she could protest.

"Ever the gentleman, aren't you?"

"My mother would've insisted on it."

"Do you miss her?"

"Every day except when I'm with you."

"Don't let me get in the way of your memories."

"No, Abilene. You're my happy memory."

"Happy memory? I call you silly pickle, and you

call me happy memory? I feel like I've done you wrong."

"Never." Lars held her hand again. "Tell me about your family."

"My family? You didn't look them up?"

"As a matter of fact, my brother said he would. But I told him I don't want to know."

"Just in case?"

"Of what?" Lars wondered what was going through Abilene's mind.

"Of things you don't want to know about my family."

"Like what, exactly?"

"Like the fact that Grandma Dupree is ninety-nine years old and she still holds the family's secret recipe for our patented hot sauce."

Lars laughed heartily. "Well, if it's patented, your government knows the secret ingredients."

"That makes two of them. Grandma and the patent office and nobody else."

"And she's going to take the information to the grave?"

"Our family has some longevity. Grandpa was almost a hundred before he got that cancer. And he lived two more years before the good Lord took him home."

"My parents both died young. What does that say about my family?"

"That you'd better live a full life because you never know when it might be time to go."

"That so?"

"Seriously, only God gives and takes lives." Abilene turned just as the sun shone into her eyes. They were really gray now in the sun.

Lars wondered how he could draw those eyes on his canvas. If only he could draw better, paint better. In fact, if only he could do everything better. Then he wouldn't be drifting through life.

Abilene stopped. She stared at the house with the wraparound second-floor porch. The ceiling fans on the balcony were not turning. The shutters were closed.

"Does anyone live there?" Lars asked.

"It's a rental." Abilene walked up the sand. "They repainted the door. It used to be dark green. Now it's navy."

"Only an artist would notice things like that."

"Anyone would, Lars."

Behind them the waves ebbed and flowed and made a din. But in front of him, that house looked quiet, like it could be a wonderful place to raise a family with kids.

Family? Kids?

What was he thinking? Lars gulped.

"Let's paint this house. Gimme my chair."

"Do I want to paint this house? Can I possibly

paint this house? I can barely paint an orange, remember?"

"Just follow my lead. I'll walk you through it. It's not that hard. We do some perspective sketching, get the frame down on paper, and then you can do whatever you want with it."

"Sounds easy."

"It'll be fun."

Lars unloaded his own easel bag. "I could paint over this yellow circle. It's sort of dried."

"How about finishing that later after you get the sand off? I have plenty of watercolor paper in various sizes today. Take your pick." Abilene pointed to her canvas carrier.

Lars filtered through the papers and picked one of the biggest ones she had. "I've never drawn anything on a paper this big."

"You don't have to take up the whole paper."

"I hear you."

They sat down for a good hour as Abilene explained perspective drawing and sketching and all the preparations they needed to take before a single drop of paint got on the paper.

"Sounds like what I missed in the first two lessons at the fort."

"Now you're all caught up."

"Good." Lars followed Abilene—copied, in fact —as she drew the house on her canvas. He found that he was a natural at this. He could draw straight lines as well as he could draw circles.

"Those are pretty straight lines, Lars."

"I wonder sometimes why I didn't take up art in secondary school."

"Secondary school? Like high school?"

"Yes. I was more into science and engineering. Same in college."

"You had an engineering degree in college?"

"Civil. Before I went to Yale for my MBA."

"Don't you draw in engineering too?"

"We use computers mostly."

"Right. So you missed out on a good old art class. Poor baby."

"I've been upgraded from silly pickle to poor baby?" Lars teased.

"It's never too late to learn. Some of my students at the fort are three times older than we are, and they draw so beautifully I'm amazed. If Grandma Dupree found out, she'd be taking up art classes too. She's quite competitive that way."

Lars watched Abilene mix her paint together.

"You don't have to use the same colors," Abilene said. "I'm using a lot of whites and grays because of the columns, but first the walls are blue."

"I prefer blue columns myself."

"Then do that. You can even change the colors of the shutters if you don't like them."

"Or make them polka-dotted."

"Uh-huh." Abilene knotted her eyebrows together.

"What?" Lars asked.

"You're sweating. Are you hot? Did you bring any water?"

"I have water. But it's kinda humid, isn't it?"

"Not for May. Go dip in the ocean if you have to. It'll cool you off."

"I didn't bring my trunks."

"You're wearing shorts. Go."

"Not unless you come with me. You're wearing shorts too."

"Sorry. Can't go with you. I'm going to paint this house."

"After a swim in the ocean."

"The wind could knock over our easels. We just set them up."

"We haven't started painting yet." Lars tried again. "If we put the easels on their sides on the sand, they won't blow over."

"We'll be wet."

"In this sun, we'll dry before lunch."

"You go ahead. I'll be right here when you come back."

"And?" Lars waited for Abilene to come up with more excuses.

"I hate swimming."

"We'll just dip in the ocean. No swimming required."

"You know you're distracting." A smile formed on Abilene's lips.

"I am?" Lars liked to be her distraction.

"We'll never finish our paintings."

"Why not?"

"We have to leave by noon to eat lunch and go to the fort for the art class. We won't be able to get much more done until tomorrow."

"So let's come back tomorrow at sunrise. We'll have more time then. Besides, we have all summer."

And then what? Lars wasn't sure. All he knew was that he didn't want his summer with Abilene to end.

CHAPTER TWENTY

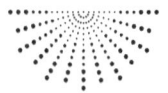

*I*t took another few weeks or so before Abilene could get back to the Rousakis Riverfront Plaza to repaint Hutchinson Island.

There was nothing she could do to repair her first oil painting that had smeared on her blouse the other morning, but she wrote it off as a draft, a sketch, an idea. It turned out to be a blessing in disguise because she decided to change her medium to oil pastels.

The three weeks with Lars had been peaceful. Abilene liked their predictable daily routine. They spent mornings painting and afternoons in art classes or working at Simon's Gallery. On a tourist visa, Lars could only volunteer, but he didn't seem to mind the lack of pay. They hung out together for lunch and dinner. Often, they walked on the waterfront.

Abilene would go home to Bradley, happy that this was her best summer ever.

This morning, their routine continued.

As per usual, Lars had tagged along with his setup at the waterfront. He was working with acrylic paint. She had promised to teach him oil painting. Someday. The day might never come. But for now, he seemed to be doing well, asking her questions now and then. He had picked up more tips from her on the beach when they painted the house. They'd finished about the same time. His was a mess, and hers was professional. It was to be expected. Her college years at SCAD hadn't been for nothing.

Lars sat closer to the water's edge while Abilene was farther back under a shady tree. From where she sat, she could see his painting.

He'd dispensed with his circle. Outgrown it, perhaps. He now painted on the entire art paper. Good for him. What he painted, though, was left to be seen. From Abilene's vantage point, it looked like another mess of colors. Very Van Gogh. Or not.

Abilene turned her attention back to her own canvas. She blended some colors together with the tip of her finger as tourists and locals filled the riverfront. She ignored the people who walked past her.

As long as they didn't knock over her easel, she was oblivious to them.

"Larson, look. A real-life street artist." A shrill British voice reached her ear.

At first she disregarded it, but the stiletto sounds stopped right next to her. "Not sure what the lady is drawing."

The blond tourist reached into her purse, snapped a twenty-dollar bill between her fingers, and dropped it into Abilene's travel mug that she had placed on the ground next to the wooden feet of her easel.

Abilene's jaw dropped as the woman grabbed her boy's hand and strutted away. Following her was a large man with a little spiral earbud coming out of one ear.

Hmm...

"Well, I guess I'll buy more coffee." Abilene snapped another pastel stick and was about to paint the blue cows into her Hutchinson Island artwork, when she heard the shrill voice call out Lars's name.

"There you are. The concierge said you'd be here." She leaned down to place a kiss on Lars's forehead, leaving a bright trace of lipstick above his right eyebrow.

Curious now, Abilene stopped working. She hated to eavesdrop, but she could hear that woman, and she could see Lars's reaction.

"Yona." Lars sounded defeated.

He caught Abilene's eye. She turned toward her painting as if she hadn't been paying attention.

Her ears burned. The way he said Yona's name sounded like they knew each other.

"I've been trying to contact you for weeks." Yona's hip-hugging skirt was only inches away from Lars's arms. "You changed your number."

"I changed it five years ago. What do you need me for?"

"To finish what we started."

"What?"

She tugged the boy's hand. The boy stepped forward with trepidation.

Abilene thought he was about four or five. He had a mop of brown curls that played in the morning Savannah sun. He was wearing a button-down shirt that looked starched and a pair of pressed shorts with a belt. On his feet were socks in green Crocs. Abilene thought maybe that was his protest. He stood ramrod straight, both arms to the side as if standing at attention.

"Larson, go ahead." The woman pushed the boy forward. "Lars, meet Larson."

"Larson?" Lars's voice sounded odd.

"Daddy?"

Abilene dropped her entire tray of oil pastels.

~

"You don't have to explain anything, Lars."

"I owe you an apology." Lars was devastated.

Yona had showed up just when his relationship with Abilene was going somewhere.

And Larson? How could he possibly be Lars's son, the similarities in names notwithstanding.

"You do." Abilene packed up her easel. "You don't mess with love."

"It was a long time ago, and no, there wasn't love between Yona and me."

"Didn't you say five years the other day? And your son is what? Four?"

"We don't know if he's my son yet." But Larson was tall for his age. All the Cargill kids were taller than their peers.

"He sure looks like you, especially his eyes."

"I didn't know Yona was pregnant when we broke up."

"Now you do."

"I told you about that time of my life. I ran away from God. I was Jonah. I was Peter. I was the prodigal son." Lars stepped in front of her. "I came back to God two years before Mother died. I haven't strayed since. I'm telling you the truth."

"Sowing and reaping, Lars. Peanuts and corn."

Lars hung his head. "I hear you. What now?"

"There's no now. There's no us. You need to study up on being a father. I need time to think. Goodbye, Lars."

It seemed Abilene had more to say, but her lips pursed. Lars couldn't read her expression. Her voice was pregnant with emotions that he decided she probably needed time to process.

"I need time to process this too. It's as much a shock to me as it is to you."

Abilene's lips quivered.

"We just started getting to know each other," he said.

"She has a child, Lars. Your child. I cannot believe he's four years old and you didn't know about him. How could that be possible? Don't you have the means to find out?"

"I never wanted to see her again. We haven't spoken since that day we broke up."

"So you do this a lot? Love someone and abandon her?"

"I told you all about it."

"You can't play with a woman's heart like that."

Lars's heart broke when he saw the shimmer in Abilene's eyes. He had never seen her cry until now.

"You should marry her and raise that child. Goodbye, Lars. Have a nice life." She ran across the street between vehicles and left Lars standing by the side of the road.

He decided not to go after her. She was hurt. He had hurt her.

Maybe he should call Pastor Flores and ask him what he should do.

Maybe he should pray and ask God what he should do instead.

What a mess I've gotten myself in.

CHAPTER TWENTY-ONE

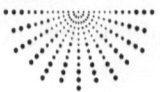

"Unbelievable." Nadine practically screamed into the phone at Abilene's ears. "What are you going to do about it?"

"Nothing. It's over between us." Abilene dried her eyes. She was sitting on a stool in the storage room of Simon's Gallery. Surrounding her were newly framed paintings that Simon would rotate out to the gallery based on his weekly or monthly exhibition theme.

"This is tough. You're going to see him at church Sunday, every Monday at Fort Pulaski, and every morning wherever you paint. I doubt if he'll stop following you around."

"I think he'll be gone soon. He has to deal with this situation."

"A four-year-old kid, huh? Is he cute like Lars?"

"Stop."

"To be fair, he did tell you about his wandering days."

"Yes, he did."

"Who knows how far he wandered."

"Stop, Nadine."

"And how many other kids he fathered."

Abilene burst into tears.

Just then what Pastor Flores had said came to her mind.

To God be true.

"Sure, even Christians can make mistakes, Abilene, but it doesn't mean you need to have anything to do with them. If you think it's time to move on, I'm with you."

Abilene's shoulders sagged. "He said he returned to God. I believed him. I so want to believe him still."

"Do you want to raise someone else's child?"

"I didn't. I don't—if Lars needs me... Oh, I don't know. I can't think."

"You need to chill and let this sit awhile. Don't do anything drastic, Abilene. Pray before you go forth. I'm sorry we didn't discover this sooner."

"Not your fault."

"This is his past catching up to him. You know my Uncle Ernest? He didn't tell his succession of wives that he had affairs throughout their marriages and fathered a bunch of kids out of wedlock. After he passed, various people showed up to claim their share of the inheritance. One drove away with a Mini Cooper, and the other, Uncle Ernest's coin collection. It happens."

Abilene didn't know whether to laugh or cry. She knew Nadine was trying to cheer her up, but the hurt was too deep. And she didn't care about Uncle Ernest, whoever he had been.

"His kisses felt real." Abilene could barely get the words out.

"They always do. I told you to hold off."

"You also came back with a clean report. Ming and you."

"Yeah. No news there about a baby out of wedlock," Nadine admitted.

Abilene was listening to her friend talk, when the storage room door creaked open.

It was Simon, the gallery owner. "Sorry. Didn't know you were in here. I need to get some paintings."

Abilene nodded. "Nadine, I'll call you later. Have to go."

"Don't forget to eat lunch," Nadine said.

My friends know me well. "I've lost my appetite."

"Nibble on something."

"Will do. Bye, Nadine." Abilene pocketed her iPhone.

Her eyes must have still been red, because Simon didn't move from where he was standing. The door was open, and they could hear the refrigerator humming in the break room in front of the storage room.

"What's the matter, Abilene?" Simon asked. He was about eighty, maybe older. He had never disclosed his age. His hair and beard were white throughout. He wore an apron that had caked clay on it. He coughed and blew his nose.

"Allergies." Simon coughed again.

"Time of year."

"Sure. What's going on? You having a pity party all by yourself?"

Abilene wondered how much to tell him. Oh well. "The guy I'm sort of going out with found out today he has a son from a previous relationship."

"I'm sorry."

"I don't know why I told you that. Not your business, really."

"I do care about the well-being of my teachers. If you're unhappy, it's going to affect your professionalism in my art classes."

"I won't let my issues get in the way."

"Is this guy in the Fort Pulaski class?" Simon asked.

"I'd rather not say."

"I should never have helped him the first day he stopped in here asking about the artist behind the *Lady and the Sea*."

Had it been two months?

Then it dawned on Abilene. Two months were simply not enough time to know someone.

Thank God all this came out in the open now before they were more involved in their relationship. She wasn't sure if they weren't already, since he had vacuumed her house the other Sunday afternoon. Crazy thing. She shouldn't have let him. He had scared Bradley the cat out the patio door with the vacuum.

Two months.

I should let him go.

"Want me to send someone to fill in for you at the fort?" Simon asked.

"I'm hoping he'll be gone before the next session."

"Just the same, let's do it. You can sub for Antonio at the Savannah Senior Living Resort on Tuesday afternoon, and he'll handle your Monday for you."

"Does Antonio know?"

"I'll tell him. He works here in the gallery on Mondays anyway, so it'll be all part of work."

"Sounds good to me. Thanks, Simon. You don't have to do anything, you know."

"And if Lars Cargill comes to the store, he'll have to get through me to get to you."

"Appreciate that."

"Now go home. Why are you even here? You don't have classes on Fridays."

"This is the closest place I could hide in."

"Don't make a habit of it." Simon walked farther into the room. "Everyone else will be hiding in here pretty soon."

Abilene chuckled. "Need any help?"

"Sure. Just getting these two paintings out to a waiting client."

The first one was an oil painting of two people dancing. The one behind it was of the same two people kissing.

Abilene lost it again.

CHAPTER TWENTY-TWO

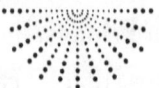

On the thirtieth floor of the Cargill Tower overlooking Canary Wharf in London, Lars found his brother wrapping up a meeting in a large conference room.

Colm Cargill, running Cargill Internet Communications alone since Lars hadn't been interested in the family business they'd inherited, remained at the end of a large teak table as his VPs left the room.

Lars had waited for him for a good half an hour, as the meeting had run overtime. He had tried to pray, but he felt distant from God. Perhaps that was his chastisement.

"Have a seat," Colm said. "I'll be with you in a sec. They want my e-signature left and right."

Lars nodded but didn't sit down. He walked over to the panoramic expanse of squeaky-clean windows overlooking parts of Canary Wharf. He could see bits of the North Dock, South Dock, and the River Thames beyond. The financial district was always crowded. Lars longed for the laid-back town of Savannah and the even more idyllic Tybee Island.

"I gather that Yona fetched you." Colm was still on his iPad.

"Who told her I was in Savannah?"

"I didn't. She's resourceful, that woman."

To Lars, it was bittersweet, this revelation that he had a four-year-old son. Effectively, it destroyed his entire future with Abilene Dupree. It made him feel more a failure than ever.

If Mother were alive, she'd be disappointed with him once again. If Father were alive, he'd give him a lecture on the golf course.

As for Colm, well, here was Colm.

Lars turned around, leaned against the windowsill, and waited. He had packed up on Thursday and flown out of Savannah that very afternoon with Yona and Larson. Larson Cargill. He still couldn't wrap his mind around that.

"You're a father." Colm swiped his iPad and placed it gently on the table. He spun his leather chair around. "That makes me an uncle."

"Congratulations, Colm. Happy day indeed."

"But you don't love Yona."

"I thought I did once. We were young."

"And stupid."

"It was a while back, Colm."

"Only five years ago. Now what, little brother?"

"I could use some advice." Lars searched the sky outside the window. The clouds had cleared and the sun came down, held off by the windows with ultra-violet protective layers.

Down below, the streets were busy. A normal day in London.

"You have a bit of a tan," Colm said from his seat.

"Should I get more? Is that your advice?" Lars tried to keep cool, but his heart was ripped apart.

"You've met a girl."

"You're reading me now?" In fact, they both read people well.

"You like this girl."

"Yes. I think I'm in love with her. Just discovering it. It was quite upsetting that Yona crashed my party."

"I can imagine. You can't undo your mistake with Yona. What's done is done, and you have to face the consequences."

"Sowing and reaping. Peanuts and corn."

"Pardon me?"

"Something Abilene said."

"Abilene." Colm smiled.

Lars had seen that slightly sly smile before. Part of it said Colm was amused, and part of it said Colm didn't think it would last.

"What's her full name?"

"Abilene Dupree." Lars wondered what Abilene's middle name was. He should know. But he didn't.

"A pretty name."

"An even prettier girl," Lars admitted.

"So what did Miss Dupree say about peanuts?" Colm locked his fingers behind his head.

Lars stepped toward the table and quoted Abilene from memory. "If you wanted corn and you planted peanuts, you can be forgiven, but you're still stuck reaping peanuts and no corn. Or vice versa."

"Such is life, Brother. Such is life." Colm closed his eyes. "I've been up half the night reading those fine prints. I'm sorry. I'm terribly tired."

"If this is a bad time, you can text me your advice later."

"No. I'm leaving for Frankfurt tonight, and I'm gone for a week. I won't have time." Colm rubbed his eyes. "Your problem is pretty easy to solve."

"Easy?"

"Yes. You and Yona are not together. The residual effect of your dalliance when you were a stupid kid is a son. You can't get rid of the son. You can offer to pay child support. You can pay for his education. You might even make a good father."

"Or a husband. I could marry Yona."

"You don't marry someone you don't love. Everyone knows that's only going to end badly."

"For Larson's sake."

"That's his name? Lars's son. Unimaginative."

"Yona named him. It seems like a branding."

"The child is not at fault."

"Sorry. You're right. I don't know how to be a father."

"Yona played the field. You told me that a long time ago."

"Yeah." Lars rued the day he had bought Yona the new boat. A few weeks later he had found her on the galley floor, naked with none other than his cousin Stuart. Turned out they had been dating for weeks while Yona was still going out with Lars. He had never felt so dirty, so used. It ended their relationship. Yona kept the boat. And Stuart.

Lars sat down. "I need a paternity test. How long do those things take?"

"Depends, I think. Could be a few days to a few weeks. Let me call our family doctor to see if she knows a lab that can expedite the process."

"I can call. You're busy, Colm."

"No problem at all. What are brothers for?"

"I love you, man."

"Love you too, Brother. And stop sleeping around."

"I don't do that anymore. Not since Yona, remember? I walk the straight and narrow now."

Colm eyed him like he didn't believe a word Lars said.

"If Larson turns out to be my son, I'll get joint custody. I'm not going to let him down."

"Good man."

Lars was happy that his older brother—only brother—seemed to be satisfied with his solution.

"What else are you doing to walk the straight and narrow? You're making yourself useful, I suppose."

"Taking up art and learning to paint."

"To what end?"

"I don't know. I enjoy it."

"Are you selling your paintings?"

"They're not good enough for sale."

"Yet?"

Lars laughed. "I'll never be like you, Colm. You pick up something, you work like crazy at it, and you end up excelling in it. I pick up something, but I might be really bad at it."

"Try and try again. Whatever you do, don't drift."

"Yep. Have an anchor. You said that."

"I did say that."

"So I joined a small church in Savannah."

Colm frowned. "Christ is your anchor, Lars, not a church. A church sometimes takes your money and does nothing of use to the cause of Christ. Too much politics. Now if you can find a church like ours, then you should be okay. How many members are in this church?"

"Riverside Chapel has ninety-five members and counting."

Colm looked stunned.

"I said it's a small church."

Colm picked up his iPad. Started swiping. "Riverside Chapel? Let's see. Savannah."

Soon, Colm's guffaws filled the room. "They meet on a riverboat?"

"Just until they can raise enough funds to build a building."

"What did I say? Money. They want your money."

"They're not like that, Colm."

"Whatever you say. So. This girl—Abilene, you said?—attends the same church?"

Lars nodded.

"A Christian, then?"

"Yes, unlike Yona."

"We don't know Yona's spirituality today, Lars. People change."

Lars buried his face in his folded arms on the table. "Why now? Years after the fact?"

"I'll have someone checking into that as well. Maybe Yona ran out of money."

"She can be high maintenance."

"But if the child is not yours, you're free and clear."

"If." Lars felt his chest constrict. He had finally found someone to love, really love, and she had slipped out of his arms because of a past he could not undo.

CHAPTER TWENTY-THREE

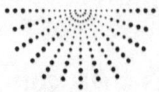

*A*bilene sat in a state of stupor throughout the church service, listening to Pastor Flores drone on about being true to God, interjected by the horns from pilot ships and visuals of sails and huge container ships outside the windows.

She didn't realize she had been looking out the windows until she heard Pastor Flores raise his voice. He was looking in her direction and saying something about seeking first the kingdom of God.

He opened his Bible and read Matthew 6:33 aloud.

But seek first the kingdom of God and His right-eousness, and all these things shall be added to you.

That verse lingered in Abilene's mind and heart

after Pastor Flores finished his sermon, the congregation sang for the last time today, and everyone was dismissed to go to lunch.

Seek first the kingdom of God and His righteousness.

And then all these things shall be added unto you.

Abilene was tossing the remainder of the Sunday programs into the recycling bin, when Nadine came over to her, Bible in hand, and a rather large tote bag over a shoulder.

"I still can't believe he did this to you." Her low voice sounded irritated.

"He said he didn't know." Abilene picked up her Bible. "Lunch somewhere?"

"And ice cream."

"I don't *need* ice cream."

"Well, I *need* ice cream." Nadine walked alongside Abilene. "Have to recover from your shocking news."

Abilene wondered what Lars Cargill was up to these days. It had been a week since he had gone home. No email. No texts. Not a word. Perhaps he was sorry about what he had done to poor ex-girlfriend and that little boy.

Perhaps he was ashamed of it all. Abilene remembered how surprised, how shocked Lars had been when the boy had shown up.

That cute little kid sure looked a whole lot like Lars.

"What are you going to do, Abilene?" Nadine asked as they walked down the ramp toward the waterfront.

"Carry on with my life."

Nadine seemed to approve. "Life after Lars. Has a good ring to it."

What else could she do, really? Abilene knew there was no way back. Lars was gone for good. Yes, the son was cute, but Abilene wasn't sure she wanted that sort of complication. Someday she'd have children of her own, but right now, she was happy with her life, thank you very much.

Then again, am I really happy?

Lunch with Nadine was quick and quiet. After having been coerced into one small scoop of ice cream, Abilene drove home alone while Nadine went back to work. Bradley greeted her at the door, meowing for his Sunday canned food. Abilene kicked off her heels and headed for the pantry.

"This is reality for you, Bradley." Abilene placed the shredded beef in a bowl in front of her cat. "You eat, sleep, play, rinse, repeat. Life is easy for you."

She changed into a summer dress, turned on the living room fan, and opened the doors to the patio.

Walking back, she passed by her collection of paintings. The *Lady and the Sea* was up against a wall.

She stopped, remembering how she and Lars had discussed not loving an illusion.

And here she was, living in a painting, in an illusion.

She stared at the painting, at the woman sitting on the beach chair reading a book.

"Lord, how do You see me?"

She already knew the answer.

God sees me through Jesus Christ, my Lord and Savior.

I'm saved and eternally secure in Christ.

"No matter what happens," she said to Bradley, passing by. He was licking his paws.

Abilene studied her watercolor painting again. The woman in the flowing summer dress had straight hair, unlike Abilene but like her sister, Arabella. Her painted woman was willowy like Mother. The way the woman sat in the chair was the way Grandma Dupree did.

But none of the features were Abilene's.

It's not me.

It had taken a once-stranger from overseas to show her that. If Lars hadn't shown up, Abilene would not have confronted herself in her paintings. Perhaps that was one good thing that had come out of their two-month-old relationship. While it had led them nowhere, God had used their time together to teach her not to project her own personal short-comings onto her paintings.

Not this way, anyway.

Abilene moved the *Lady and the Sea* to her front door and leaned it against the coat closet door. She had kept the painting long enough. In the morning, she would take it to Simon's Gallery and put it up for sale. She would give all the proceeds to Riverside Chapel.

CHAPTER TWENTY-FOUR

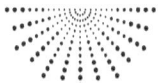

*T*he verdict was in.

Lars was so relieved at the outcome of the DNA tests that he dropped on his knees right there in the living room of his London flat, the Bible in his hand falling to the plush carpet with a small thud.

Loudly, he thanked almighty God for having rescued him yet again. He knew that this time it could have gone either way.

The principle of sowing-and-reaping happened regardless of whether he was a Christian or not. It was sort of like a law of nature.

He knew he had made a lot of mistakes in his life, and this one was by far one of the biggest.

Rather than a reprieve, Lars chided himself for

being that careless. He had taken love lightly, mixed it with pleasure, and had paid for it in painful regret five years later.

Somehow he felt like David. Though the famous king had committed adultery and Lars hadn't, sin was sin.

Lars knew God took sin so seriously that he had imposed a death penalty on sin, a penalty that Lars couldn't possibly pay.

In the muck and mire of his life, his mother had come to see him one fine day some three years ago. She had just come off chemotherapy. Her hair was gone, though her wig was becoming.

She had come to his flat to read one single verse in the Bible to him. He had listened only because he knew his time with his mother was running out.

That day, he remembered why his Lord and Savior, Jesus Christ, came to earth.

It was because of him!

How could he forget that Jesus had paid the penalty for his sins? Death was no more. Only life.

And he had ruined that abundant life with lascivious living. It was by the grace of God that he hadn't contracted any venereal disease from Yona, whom he had to break up with when he found out she hadn't been monogamous for the two years he'd been sleeping in her flat at night.

Still on his knees, he reached for the Bible on the carpet. He opened it. A big and bold signature was on the title page.

Kayla Modipe-Cargill.

Mother had since passed away, but she had left Lars her Bible as part of her will. The Bible had been in his mother's family for decades.

Also on the page, Mother had written some words in her flawless handwriting. Lars read those two lines aloud. "God has given me grace after grace. Mercy after mercy."

I miss you, Mother.

Still on his knees, he wept openly.

~

*P*erfect golf weather in County Antrim had brought Lars's brother to his favorite exclusive course in all the world, but it meant Lars had to go there as well if he wanted to know what Colm had to say to him.

This was the fifth day they were on the golf cart heading for the links, when Colm finally broached the subject Lars had been waiting for all week.

"Good stock," Colm said.

"You made me caddy for a week just to talk about company shares?" Lars knew there was more.

There was always more with Colm. In many ways, he was like Dad. Colm had taken after Dad, and Lars had taken after Mother.

"I want you to know that I approve." Colm parked the cart.

"Approve?"

"Of her." Colm swiped his iPhone. "I'm forwarding you the report."

Her?

Report?

"What in the world, Colm?" Lars tried not to be judgmental, since his brother had rescued him many times in his life, but this was getting a bit too cryptic, too much.

All he wanted to do was go home to Savannah—

Home?

He had just been there for about two months. How could he consider it his home?

His iPhone pinged. He read the email. Attached was a thirty-some-page background check on none other than one Abilene Jasmine Marguerite Dupree.

"You didn't." Lars shook his head. "You're like Nadine."

"Nadine? Nice name. Who's that?" Colm walked around the cart to get his golf clubs.

Lars stayed in the cart. He scrolled down the

report. Of course he wanted to read it. Curiosity had gotten the better of him though he was still miffed that Colm had done this without his knowledge.

"I paid a big sum for the expedited research, but you don't need to thank me for it, Lars. Just consider it my wedding gift to you."

"Wedding what?" Lars was lost in thought.

He scrolled through Abilene's entire family tree all the way to 1620 Jamestown through to their intertwining French, Spanish, Native American, and European genetic mixes, all culminating in the force that apparently moved mountains: Marguerite Dupree, otherwise known as Mama Dupree, Grandma Dupree, Hot Sauce Dupree, or simply, Hot Dupree.

"It's all business to you, isn't it?" Lars asked.

Colm waited. "Where's my caddy?"

Lars ignored him. "You're thinking of investing in hot sauce?"

"Already done."

Oh, Abilene was a cutie pie at three years old with her curls. Lars scrolled some more. There were her mother and father, and gobs of uncles and aunts. Right in the middle of the family reunion album was Grandma Dupree upon whose lap Abilene was squirming.

Lars felt he was invading her privacy.

If she were to show him these photos, it would've been all right.

But not like this. Not on the sly. Not through a private investigator or Colm's connections to MI5 and MI6 and Scotland Yard and Interpol and the FBI.

"No." He exited the file without reading the rest of it. He deleted it from his email account.

"No what?"

"She'll tell me what she wants to tell me. I won't dig into her life like this. It's an invasion of privacy."

"Is it, Lars? If you had done this with Yona, you wouldn't have moved in with her the year she was messing with your heart."

"Heart?" Lars remembered Abilene saying something about hearts too.

"What do you know about heart?" Lars was eye to eye with his brother now.

He couldn't get angry with Colm. Not ever. He knew Colm was trying to help him, but his ways bypassed the heart. It was all mind and no soul.

"I know enough."

Lars didn't want to say more. "I'd better go. I waited five days for you to tell me what you said was important—"

"This is important."

"I missed seeing her for five more days because of this."

"Five days. What's the big deal? That report could save your life."

"And fortune?"

"Well, the Dupree family could go toe to toe with the Cargills, but we're not in the same business. We do software and they do hot sauce."

As Colm's friends trickled in, Lars decided to let the matter rest. This was Colm. This was how Colm did things.

"I've got your back, little brother." Colm's voice cracked. He might be only eleven months older than Lars, but he seemed older than that now.

"You don't have to fill Dad's shoes. I love you, regardless."

"I love you too, Lars."

Lars was visibly moved, but he didn't want to hug Colm. Colm wouldn't have expected it and it would be awkward in front of all those oncoming golf carts.

"Hey, thank you for checking into Abilene." Lars laughed. "Good stock, you say?"

"I didn't know how else to say it."

It was an admission from Colm. Maybe there was hope for him yet.

"Come see me in Savannah sometime." Lars lifted the golf bag. It was heavy, but that was the deal. He had given Colm his word that he'd be his caddy for the day, and that was the way it went. "My house is your house."

"We'll see what your Abilene says about that."

Your Abilene.

Lars liked the sound of that.

CHAPTER TWENTY-FIVE

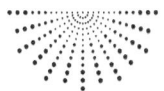

*T*he wings of the brown pelican were so close to the cresting waves that Abilene thought they would skim the surface of the ocean. They didn't. The pelican swooped down, opened its bucket beak, and scooped up a fish.

Abilene wished she'd caught the entire scene on camera. Etched in her mind, the instant replay brought forth more details. The shades of brown on the pelican's wings, the powerful beak, the hunger for food, the successful hunt.

As the pelican flew away, Abilene decided that her next painting of the Atlantic Ocean would be of the brown pelicans up and down this coast.

The late July dawn had left the sky, and in its place a glorious blue expanse stretched above the ocean and over Abilene. God had painted the subtlest shades of sky blue there, the cirrus clouds an easy brushstroke from heaven.

Abilene stared awhile, then returned to her painting.

The smudge, he'd called it.

She left the woman in red standing at the water's edge. She could never be replaced. That red dress against a wash of ocean blue behind her and sandy beige beneath her feet were too bright to be washed down.

Abilene focused on the foreground, trying to remember the hair color, the smile, the contours of his neck and shoulders—

"That doesn't look like me."

Lars.

Abilene shrieked.

The bristles on her brush went askew, and brown paint streaked across her painting at an unnatural angle.

She spun around.

Lars Cargill leaned around her, his eyes on the painting. "Tsk-tsk. Another smudge. You need to learn to paint inside the lines, Abilene."

His aftershave mingled with fresh soap made Abilene giddy.

She cleared her throat. "I thought you'd be married by now."

"Not to the wrong girl, I'm not." His eyes caught hers.

"But your son?"

"My cousin's son."

Abilene couldn't speak.

Not his child!

"The lab took longer than expected, and Yona wanted it retested. So did Stuart. I was going to adopt the child when they fought bitterly on the matter."

"How kind of you."

Not his child!

Abilene still couldn't believe it.

"Finally, we let the solicitors duke it out. They finished signing the papers a week ago, and the large bill is on the way to poor Yona and Stuart. I wanted to fly out then, but my brother had something he wanted me to see. I had to wait for him. Lost another five days."

"You could've just texted me. Saved some money."

"I had to see you in person. I missed you, Abilene."

"Me too, but I don't want you to spend frivolous money on account of me."

"Then you don't want to know that I couldn't get a flight out due to the summer season. My brother let me use his jet."

"You flew here on a charter jet?"

"My brother doesn't charter. It's his own jet." Lars shrugged, like it was nothing. "Poor little Larson now has a name change."

"Larson's a cute name." Abilene tried to keep cool. The sun was up in the sky, it was getting as warm as July could be, and she was beginning to sweat in her sundress. She usually didn't.

"Not to Stuart. He doesn't want his son named after the *other* man. The kid is now Stuart McGilverney Cargill VIII."

Abilene wiped sweat off her forehead.

Not his child!

Lars fished out a perfectly folded embroidered handkerchief and handed it to her as if he did it all the time. Abilene had never seen that handkerchief before. Was this the real Lars here? The gentleman with the hanky?

Somehow she should've expected it.

Even when Lars was here in May and June, he'd been the perfect British gentleman, or her idea of one, at the very least. He had not forced himself on her or pressured her to go out with him. Grandma Dupree would've said he was a good Christian man. Mom and Dad would've agreed.

Abilene dabbed her forehead with the hand-kerchief.

Lars held out his hand. "Come. Let me show you something."

"What?"

"A surprise."

Hesitantly, Abilene followed him. They walked on the wet sand barefoot, the saltwater cool around Abilene's ankles. It was as if the three weeks of separation never happened. It was as if it were only last week that they'd walked this way toward—

Lars stopped right in front of that house with the wraparound porch. That one with the wrong color on the door.

He held Abilene's hand as they walked up the beach, dry sand sticking to their wet feet.

Standing in front of the prettiest house on Tybee Island, Abilene remembered the two days, maybe three, they'd spent painting this. Lars had copied her painting somewhat. His colors had more punch, while her painting had been more pastel.

They'd finished about the same time, then dipped in the ocean again in their tee shirts and shorts as their paintings dried in the June sun.

Jangling keys broke her muse.

Lars dangled the keys in front of Abilene. "Our house. We'll sign the paperwork later for the deed."

"What?" Abilene's jaw dropped.

"You don't like it? Maybe we can repaint the door."

"What—what have you done?"

"I bought you the house you wanted. Grandma Dupree said you would never buy it yourself. Something about being a tightwad."

"What did you just call—wait a minute. You talked to Grandma Dupree?" No, no, no. Grandma Dupree had all sorts of ideas, including marrying off all her grandchildren pronto so she could hand down her secret hot sauce recipes to the next generations.

"Uh-huh. She's really nice. I also talked to your mom and dad and your brother, Dante."

"How did you get their numbers?" Abilene was really sweating now.

This was too personal. He had talked to her family. She didn't even know whether she wanted to continue going out with him.

"I went to see them."

"You went to New Orleans?"

Lars nodded.

"I thought you said you flew here as quickly as you could."

"Right. I flew here as quickly as I could by way of Grandma Dupree's house. She insisted I go to church with the family, so I stayed another day. Then she insisted I try out the hot sauce in her new restaurant, and next thing you know, lunch was over, and I got in last night and crashed in the hotel."

"You poor thing."

"They gave me their blessings."

Abilene shook her head. "To buy me this house?"

"Not that. This." He dropped on both knees on the sand.

He went down with such force that Abilene was startled. She tried to help him up. "Are you okay?"

"More than okay." A ring appeared. "Abilene Dupree, will you marry me?"

"No."

"What?"

"No."

"Why?"

"I will only say yes to that question once in my lifetime."

Lars lifted the ring. It sparkled in the Georgian sun. "So say yes."

"No."

"Because?"

"We have something to clear up between us."

"Oh?" Lars's voice was tinged with confusion.

"The woman in my painting." Was Lars in love with her or the *Lady and the Sea*? "The one you pined over?"

"What about her?"

"I have to know."

"I have the real you, Abilene. What more could I ask for? Besides, that was just a painting."

"But you still want to know who that is."

"If you want to tell me, I'm listening."

Abilene drew a deep breath and folded her arms in front of her. "It's not me. The lady is my grandmother, my mother, my sister."

Lars grinned. His dimple looked cute when he grinned.

Don't be distracted!

Abilene cleared her throat. "All the over-achievers in the Dupree family."

"Oh. But you're an amazing artist. None of them is."

"Well..."

"I'm not marrying them. I'm marrying you. I have no doubt in my mind you're the one." Lars reached for Abilene's left hand. She didn't pull away. He lifted her fingers.

"I want to see you as God sees you," he said. "Love you as He loves you."

"And I you."

"Say yes."

"Oh, all right."

"That's not a yes. Say the word, Abilene."

"Yes, silly pickle, I'll marry you."

"I guess I can live with that." He slid the

diamond-encrusted engagement ring onto her finger. It fitted perfectly.

Abilene was surprised. "How did you—oh, I should've guessed. Grandma Dupree."

"She knows all about you."

"Uh-oh. What did she say about me?"

"Lots of stuff."

"Like what?"

"I'll tell you later." Lars stood. "Now I have more important things to—"

Abilene reached him first. His lips were warm. His arms were gentle and caring.

Next thing she knew, he lifted her up and they were heading toward the ocean.

"What are you doing, Lars?"

"Celebrating."

"Put me down!"

He laughed.

"I'm going to lose the ring in the ocean!"

"I'll get you another one. Besides, it's insured."

Abilene went splashing into the water. Not to be outdone, she reached up for him, grabbed his shirt, and pulled him down into the waves.

Their mirth and joy mingled with the crashing waves and squawking seabirds above.

CHAPTER TWENTY-SIX

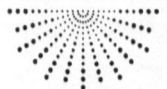

*A*bilene's mom called her before she had a chance to process through everything that had just happened to her. The ring, the house, the proposal, the man.

Yes, the man.

"I don't want an engagement party, Mom." Dragging the rolling art case behind her, loaded with watercolor paper, paintbrushes, and paint tubes for her ten students in the tree class, Abilene crossed Bull Street and made her way to Johnson Square.

She was early by half an hour and was in no hurry, but the more Mom talked, the faster Abilene walked.

"Your dad would be so disappointed," Mom said. "How about a small one?"

"Small?" Small to Mom would mean a hundred people at least.

"Cap Juluca could handle our crowd."

Anguilla. Wow. Her parents were sparing no expenses for their youngest daughter.

"A small crowd, right, Mom?"

"Maybe fifty people."

"Fifty? Really?"

"Or sixty. Seventy. Make that a hundred. Or two."

"Mom."

"You and Lars would need two separate villas. I'll call to see if we can get enough villas for everyone."

"Mom!"

"Ophelia would be disappointed if her family isn't invited."

"Ophelia is your second cousin twice removed. Couldn't you tell her this engagement party—only an engagement party—is just for immediate family?"

"She'd want to come."

"I haven't seen her since I was five or six. I don't even remember what she looks like."

Mom ignored her and rambled on about other relatives who would feel slighted if they did not receive invitations to both the engagement party and the wedding.

Abilene could not remember any of her friends hosting both events.

"Mom, inviting a hundred people to Anguilla and putting them all up in villas seems extravagant to me. Besides, I'm already engaged."

"It's an announcement."

"So tell them all on Facebook. It's free. Give the money to missions." She paused. She knew her mom didn't want to hear it, but she had to say it. "Lots of hungry kids to feed. Lots of hurting people to minister to."

"I was afraid you'd say that, Abilene."

Abilene rounded the monument of Nathanael Greene from the Revolutionary War. The war had happened decades after Johnson Square had been designed in 1733, one year after General Oglethorpe settled near the bluff, though none of the traces of the original settlers were here now.

Today, the entire square was overrun with tall live oak trees, the subject of her art class today.

"Well, my precious daughter, it's your happy day."

"Isn't that supposed to be my wedding day?"

"We haven't gotten to your wedding day yet. We're just getting started with the engagement party."

"That's what I was afraid of."

Abilene reached the spot designated for the one-afternoon tree workshop. She set her art case upright. Rivulets of sweat trickled down from under her baseball cap, rolled down her face, and onto her neck.

"About the wedding..."

"Mom, I have to go. I have an art class to teach, remember?"

Abilene was the only one standing there under the imposing canopy of green, lush, healthy oak trees with sprawling branches covering the entire sky above her.

"Your cousin chartered an entire cruise ship for seven days, and had her wedding on the Inside Passage through the glaciers," Mom said.

"How could anyone forget?" It had been so chilly in July that Abilene had to wear a goose-down jacket throughout the outdoor wedding on the top deck of the cruise ship. The backdrop had been stunning though. Blue glaciers falling into the cold, cold sea. Seals and mountain goats flanking the eroding mountains.

"Seven days of wedding feasts." Mom remembered too.

"That's Arabella. That's not me."

"You like land and sea. How about something coastal? Mykonos?"

"No."

"Santorini?"

"No."

"Got it! Venice, dear. Lots of water there."

"No."

Mom sighed. Heavily. "All right. Where do you want your wedding, Abilene?"

"Pastor Flores had his wedding on a riverboat."

"A—a riverboat, you said?" Mom asked.

"Yeah. I know it doesn't sound like a cruise ship, but it's small and intimate."

"Small. How many people can it seat, dear?"

"Well, it can hold about twelve hundred passengers. Plenty of room for everyone."

"Everyone would want to come. I'm sure all of Grandma Dupree's nephews and nieces, plus all of your friends, and everybody."

Everybody.

Abilene opened up her art case, found her easel, and snapped it into place with one hand. From this vantage point she could see the rest of Bull Street all the way down to the Savannah City Hall, its multiple floors, and the impressive gold-leaf dome on top.

"Maybe we should elope." Abilene felt someone touch her waist. She recognized the warmth.

She turned to find Lars, wide eyed, questioning. He must've heard the tail end of their conversation.

Elope.

He wrapped his arms around her nonetheless.

Abilene was still on the phone.

"No, Abilene." Mom sounded horrified. "We can't be the only ones witnessing your wedding."

"We? Mom, if we elope, it'll be just Lars and me."

"Sweetheart, your dad and I would want to come."

"You can't—what?"

"Grandma Dupree and Arabella would want to be there too."

"It wouldn't be an elopement if everybody comes." Abilene shook her head as Lars continued to kiss her neck. She wondered if he could hear what Mom said.

"Once in a lifetime, Abilene. You need to make the wedding spectacular."

"I agree with you, Mrs. Dupree," Lars said into the phone.

"Is that you, Lars? Thank you. Talk some sense into my daughter, will you?"

"Yes, ma'am."

"Have to run," Abilene said. "Class starting."

"We'll talk soon, dear."

"Sure thing, Mom." *Click.*

She wrinkled her nose at Lars. "Are you colluding with Mom?"

"She's right, you know. A wedding should be spectacular. A celebration to tell the world we're getting married for life."

For life.

"Invite everyone. No big deal." He kissed her forehead. "But if you want a small wedding, I'm fine with that too. Either way."

"You seem calm about it."

"As long as I'm marrying you, I have no complaints. I thank God for you every day, and we're going to get married one way or another." He leaned down and grazed his lips against hers.

"Are we supposed to draw you doing that?" It was the tiniest little voice.

Abilene stepped back from Lars. A pair of cute bright eyes looked up at her. In the little girl's hands were color pencils and a tear-out from some art pad.

"Hello, sweetie," Abilene said. "Are you in my art class today?"

The girl nodded, her red curls bouncing all around her forehead.

"We're going to draw and color trees today. Where's your mommy?"

She pointed to where a thirtysomething woman was setting up her easel. There was nothing on the Simon's Gallery class page that said childcare was provided for the adult art class. Abilene hadn't brought a kid's easel.

But she remembered when she was about that age, learning to draw. If anyone had stopped her from doing so, she wondered what might have happened today.

"I have a picnic blanket. Would you like to sit on that to draw?" Abilene reached for her art case.

"Yes!"

Abilene unfolded the blanket. Lars helped her put it on the ground next to the girl's mother.

"I have to go," Lars said. "I have a meeting in fifteen minutes."

He didn't say where, and Abilene didn't ask. If he had wanted to tell her, he would.

"Are you going to take another art class sometime?" she asked instead.

"Yep. Your next class."

"Acrylic?"

"Whatever it is, I'll be there." He walked backward while facing her, as if he was loathe to leave her.

Seemed he was heading for River Street. Back to his hotel? A meeting, he'd said. What meeting?

Abilene was somewhat disappointed that Lars didn't stay for the tree class, but the diamond on her ring finger glinting in the afternoon sun appeased her. She'd see Lars at dinner, anyway.

And tomorrow morning when they met with the interior decorator and renovation contractor.

More tardy people arrived, and soon Abilene was busy teaching them how to sketch and paint trees.

CHAPTER TWENTY-SEVEN

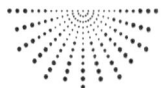

*L*ars bounded down the brick stairs to the grimy cobblestones, where cars were parked and pedestrians wove in and out. River Street was crowded as usual this first Friday of August.

Tonight there would be fireworks, and he couldn't wait to tell Abilene another surprise when they met for dinner. She'd seen the fireworks before but not combined with some great news that he had for her.

It all depended on this meeting with Simon Kowalski. At half past two o'clock in the afternoon, Lars found the gallery owner at the back of the long store, taking pictures of a painting. The back of the painting faced Lars, and he couldn't see what was so mesmerizing to Simon that he took many photographs of it.

"Hi there." Simon kept at it. "Come see this for the last time before it goes to a private collection."

Lars took two steps toward Simon and came to a complete stop.

Lady and the Sea.

"Is this her biggest original?" Lars asked.

"Yep. This is the first painting she did. She replicated this onto smaller canvases, one of which I sold to you last year."

Lars remembered. But how did Abilene capture the same wispy smile in the woman? "Where has this one been?"

"Abilene kept it. She doesn't want it anymore."

"How much are you listing this one for?"

"Listed. It's sold, Lars. Yesterday."

"For?"

"Eleven thousand. I asked for nine, but two collectors wanted it. The higher bidder won."

"Makes sense." Lars couldn't help it. He was sad. Could this be the same painting hidden at the back of the coat closet in Abilene's apartment? The one she didn't want him to see?

"May I ask a question?"

"Yes, you may."

"Do you think the lady in the painting is Abilene herself?"

Simon laughed so hard that his stomach began to jiggle, and so loudly that he began to cough. He kept pointing to the table near Lars until the latter realized he was asking for the bottled water. After gulping down the water, Simon cleared his throat.

"You should have that looked at," Lars suggested.

"The painting?"

"No. Your throat."

"That's what my wife said."

"I concur with her. How long have you been coughing?"

"Ages. Allergies. Year round."

Lars felt sorry. "If this is the wrong time to have a meeting, I can come back another day."

"No. No. It'll be the same tomorrow, next week, the week after. Abilene dropped off some new paintings last week."

"How many?"

"Five or six. Want to see? They're on the way to my office."

"You bet I do." Lars followed Simon on the brief tour. Abilene's paintings, some watercolor, some oil, some acrylic, and some oil pastels, were scattered all over. No Hutchinson Island though, but—

There it is.

"That'd better fetch a good price for you,

Simon." Lars pointed to the riverboat. "That guy there. That's me."

"Is that right?" Simon ran his fingers through his beard. "Do you want the painting? Abilene is going to give the proceeds of all these paintings to her church's fundraising program. Can't blame them for not wanting to be in a riverboat forever."

She's giving away her profits. "Do artists generally get fifty percent of retail?"

Simon nodded. "Pretty much."

"Riverside Chapel is my church too."

"Is it? Then you're invested. Painting's five thousand dollars if you want it."

Lars made a mental calculation. That would be slightly over three thousand British pounds. "I'll take it."

"Sold!" Simon coughed again.

He was too close to the painting.

"I'll get it." Lars didn't want Simon's spits and sneezes to be all over his new painting.

He wanted this painting. He still remembered the day in May he had met Abilene, the day she had painted him into the picture because he had been standing in her line of sight, talking to his brother on the phone and picking up a brochure from Riverside Chapel. He recalled the conversation with his brother. Colm had reminded him not to drift through life.

Well, he had stopped drifting.

And found a new home.

Simon entered his office, which was a hole in the wall at the other end of the long hallway. It was sparse with only one photo hung on the wall, that of his wife and two kids. Lars didn't know Simon had kids. He never talked about them and didn't bring them up in conversations. Perhaps they lived elsewhere and didn't come home often. He hoped they called their parents once in a while, at least.

"Have a seat." Simon tented his fingers on the table and went straight to the point. "I talked it over with my wife, and we decided we don't want to sell a part of the gallery."

Lars tried to remain stoic. "No?"

"We had a third partner once, and it didn't work out." Simon leaned forward. "What we want to do is sell the whole gallery. Xian and I need a change of scenery. We want to move to Arizona or some place dryer. Maybe my allergies would go away if we weren't living among so many trees. I'm allergic to them all, did you know?"

Lars shook his head.

Simon wants to sell his entire gallery.

"We're eighty and not getting any younger. We want to travel a bit, see the kids and grandkids."

Ah, they do exist.

"When do you need to know?"

"ASAP."

"Abilene is teaching a class right now. We're meeting for dinner. I want to talk it over with her then. See what she thinks. I'll text you to let you know where we're at."

CHAPTER TWENTY-EIGHT

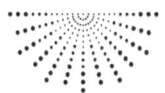

"I don't know if I want to own an art gallery, Lars," Abilene said over shrimp fried rice. Across the table, Lars was navigating his chopsticks in the hot noodle soup. "I know Simon hasn't shown any profits in three years."

"I'll have my accountant look into it before we do anything."

"Why would you want to buy a gallery to begin with?" Abilene knew that Lars was interested in art, but as a hobby, she had thought.

"To put your paintings in it."

"Or because you feel sorry for Simon?" Abilene dabbed her lips with the paper napkin.

"Both?"

"Dad and Grandma Dupree said never to make

business decisions based on emotions. It'll always cost more."

"The gallery is pretty cheap." Lars named the price. "Cheaper than the beach house."

"It's not worth much, then."

"I wouldn't put it that way. I think I'll enjoy being a gallery owner more than being an artist. I can put my MBA to good use."

"Your MBA from Oxford."

"Thanks to Ming's investigative prowess." Lars finished his soup. "What else do you know about me?"

"Nothing you haven't already told me. Tell me, Lars. What are your long-term plans if you buy Simon's Gallery?"

"For one, the building itself is narrow and long. I don't like that. Do you?"

"Simon had no choice. It was all he could afford." Abilene ate the last shrimp. "It's an old building not meant to be a gallery. It used to be a long, narrow shop."

"The shop next door used to be part of the gallery."

Abilene nodded. "A few years back. When his daughter married and moved away, he sold it."

"But River Street is where we need to be if we run a business."

"We? I'm not totally sold on buying a gallery."

Abilene pointed to her iPhone. "Fireworks in twenty minutes."

"We'd better go." Lars waved to a server.

Five minutes later, they had paid for their meals and were holding hands while crossing River Street, heading toward the waterfront, where the fireworks display could be seen clearly over the Savannah River.

Lars pulled Abilene toward him. She eased into his chest. Above them the fireworks lit up the sky just as they did every first Friday of the month.

"What if we run the gallery for three years?" Lars whispered in Abilene's ears. "If it doesn't work, we shut it down, sell the building, and move on."

"Shhh. I'm watching the fireworks."

Then he did it again. "It could be my day job."

Abilene's lips were at his ears. "You could lose all your money."

"I won't lose *all* my money."

"We should only put expendable cash into that gallery."

"We?" Lars's eyes searched hers.

"Expendable cash. Agreed?" Abilene stopped paying attention to the fireworks above her. She could see them in Lars's eyes as she faced away from the river.

"Agreed."

Abilene looked past Lars to the row of shops

lining River Street facing the waterfront. Those shops and restaurants were in a prime zone because they were visible. Simon's Gallery was tucked away at an obscure corner two or three blocks from here. Unless it showcased famous artists, its discoverability by the tourists flocking Savannah was nil.

"What if we move Simon's Gallery to River Street?" Abilene asked.

Slowly, realization emerged on Lars's face. He turned around. Now both of them were facing away from the fireworks. "I like that idea, Abilene. Love your business acumen."

"I'm an art major."

"Even artists have to make a living."

"Good point."

"Do you think any of those stores is for sale?" Lars asked.

"We can ask Sabine to find us one. But first, let's pray about this. Pray for wisdom and timing."

"I can't agree more. God's best is what I want."

CHAPTER TWENTY-NINE

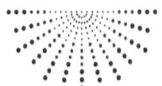

*A*bilene was near tears. The more Sabine Wei, real estate agent and interior designer, and Tobias Vega, the contractor from Brooks Renovations, talked, the worse she felt.

The first time she'd seen the inside of this beach house was the day Lars had proposed to her. Last week. Monday morning.

The house had been a mess. Tumbled furniture, torn fixtures, trash, grime, and graffiti were every-where throughout the house. Clogged toilets, broken faucets, unhinged doors. It was as if the house had been vandalized or the previous tenants had been destructive. Maybe both.

Abilene wondered now about that navy door that faced the ocean. Perhaps it hadn't just been repainted. Perhaps it was a new door, replacing an old one too destroyed to be rehung.

One week later, everything that could be thrown out had been thrown out, and what was left was still bad. There was structural damage the home inspector hadn't seen. Termite problems notwithstanding, the house was literally sinking into the sand.

"We might as well torch this place and rebuild from scratch." Abilene was upset. It didn't help that her monthlies started last night. It sometimes put her through an emotional wringer. "The house looks so pretty from the outside."

"It still does." Lars stroked her shoulder. "We'll fix whatever needs to be fixed."

Tobias agreed. "Let's start with the foundation. First thing we need to do is stabilize it. You see the floor is sagging here"—he pointed to the floor with his iPad—"and here and here. Oh, and here."

"Thank God we've made provisions for this in the contract." Abilene held Lars's hand. "Thank you, Sabine, for insisting on the home inspection."

"Anytime." Sabine's baby bump showed through her loose outfit. She was several months into her pregnancy.

Abilene wondered what it felt like to carry a child, to have a child, to raise the child.

Meanwhile... "This house could wash out to sea."

"We'll shore up this house built on shifting sand," Tobias said.

"And build the house on solid rock," Lars added. He swiped his iPhone and unearthed Matthew 7:26-27. "On sand, it's pretty bad."

> *But everyone who hears these sayings of Mine, and does not do them, will be like a foolish man who built his house on the sand: and the rain descended, the floods came, and the winds blew and beat on that house; and it fell. And great was its fall.*

"We do get hurricanes this side of the Atlantic," Abilene said.

"But not today!" Lars and Tobias said in unison.

"What's with you guys?" Sabine stepped in between Tobias and Lars. "Take this seriously, will you?"

"How long is the reno going to take?" Abilene needed some fresh air.

She walked outside to the balcony. The sun was warming up. Another humid July day on the coast of Georgia.

"Like Toby said, we have to get the foundation straightened out." Sabine joined her on the balcony. "I'll call around today to see what everybody's schedule looks like. Once the foundation looks good, it should last fifty or more years."

"Good."

"I don't expect them to take more than a month. Then Toby and I can move on the reno. How long it takes depends on how much you want done."

"The entire house needs to be gutted."

"I agree. Could be two to three months, if we get cranking after they fix the foundation. We might get you in by Christmas."

"Christmas?"

"If there are no unexpected delays."

Abilene started to lean against the balcony railing and then thought better of it. Inside the house, Lars and Tobias were talking about something she couldn't hear. She caught the tail end of it. Lars had invited Tobias to church on Sunday.

Abilene turned her attention back to Sabine. "Brooks Reno is based on St. Simon's Island. Is Tobias coming up here every day?"

"He supervises projects up and down the coast. Not to worry. He has a branch here with several crews doing work in the area. Savannah, Richmond, Tybee."

"If you trust him, I trust him, Sabine."

"I do."

"Good enough for me." Abilene nodded, satisfied. "When can we see your ideas and options?"

"My team is working on it now. How about Friday? That'll give us three days to tidy up the presentation. We can meet at my office." Sabine gave Abilene a hug. "Don't worry. Everything will work out. God will work things out."

Abilene nodded. "The transformation will be spectacular, right?"

"For sure." Sabine glowed. "When's your wedding?"

"We haven't set a date yet on account of this house."

"After Christmas is a safer bet," Sabine suggested.

"Right. We'll probably have to wait until things thaw out a bit." Abilene motioned for Lars to join them. "What do you think of a winter wedding?"

"Cold. Let's try spring?" Lars wrapped his arms around Abilene.

Abilene liked it when Lars and she came up with the same ideas. "March or April if we can book Riverside Chapel?"

"Sounds good to me, although that's a good eight or nine months away," Lars said. "I can't stay at the hotel that long."

"I can help you there," Sabine said. "I know some affordable rentals."

Affordable? Abilene didn't say a word, but anything was affordable to both Lars and her. She figured she was more frugal than Lars, but he could hold his own. For example, he only rented a compact car to get around town, when he could've easily rented a sports car. He stayed at a decent hotel that wasn't even rated five stars. He could have gone palatial on his hotel accommodations, but he didn't.

My kind of guy.

And yet.

Yet, he had gone and done something Abilene wouldn't have done. He had dropped two million dollars into this dump.

And he decided to buy Simon's Gallery, knowing that art galleries were not always profitable.

In both cases, he had done it for her.

For me.

Abilene stepped on a creaky floorboard as she headed for the stairs. "Let's see that inspection report again, Lars."

Before Lars could say anything, the entire railing fell off the stairs and crashed down onto the first floor below. Abilene couldn't scream even if she wanted to. Her heart was stuck somewhere up her throat, and she couldn't breathe.

"Might be why you got this house on the cheap. Can't believe this passed inspection." Tobias laughed all by himself as he walked past them. "Just step where I step."

They all followed him, single file, all the way down the stairs and out the door.

Once she was on the porch, Abilene screamed and ran all the way to the ocean. She tripped and fell into the water again. This time the Atlantic served a purpose. It masked her tears.

Hadn't Lars read the inspection report before he bought the house?

Okay, Lord, I'll try not to blame him.

Abilene was equally to blame, as she had signed the papers too. She should have read everything twice before she picked up the pen. She had trusted Lars.

And she had been giddy.

I'm getting married!

She stood up in the water, caught her breath, and found Lars staring at her from the shoreline. His eyebrows dropped, his face was contorted, as if he had caused her a great irrevocable harm.

Lord, please give me something encouraging to say to this man I love.

Abilene waded back to shore.

Lars helped her out of the water. His shoulders sagged. "I'm so sorry."

"Don't be."

"My wedding gift is a wreck."

"Only the house is. We bought the view. This is prime oceanfront real estate. Almost a whole acre. A steal of a deal, if you ask me."

"I suppose." Lars nodded.

Abilene's heart dissolved. There was so much pain in his face that she couldn't possibly add more hurt. She touched his stubbled chin. They stood there quietly, wondering what to do.

"God has a way out of this, I'm sure," Lars finally said.

"Or *through* this." Abilene managed a smile. "For better, for worse, remember?"

Some sort of light returned to Lars's eyes. "There's a reason I'm in love with you, Abilene."

"A reason? Like, only one?"

"You know what I mean. So. Moving forward. Do we believe in God?"

"Always, Lars."

"Do we believe He can fix this?"

"God can fix anything." Abilene held Lars's hands. "In this case, He might be leading us to start over. Afresh. Anew."

"Right. Our relationship is stronger than the foundation of any house." Lars seemed to be looking for a hug.

"I'm drenched. You'll get wet." Her summer dress clung to her body. She'd dry in the July sun sooner than she could get a sunburn, but right now, she'd get Lars's shirt wet too if they stepped any closer to each other.

"I don't care." He drew her into his chest.

Abilene felt nothing but love for him.

"Our marriage will be anchored in Christ," Lars declared.

Was that a promise from Lars or a statement of faith?

Lars opened his mouth to say more, but Abilene stopped him with her lips. He seemed to relax as the kiss grew deeper.

As soon as he came up for air, he said, "We can't build our home on moving sand."

"But we can build it on a rock." Abilene pointed. "We have that stretch of land all the way to the road."

"Right." Lars put on his sunglasses.

"The closer to the road we put the house, the more beach we have." Abilene looked for her sandals.

"Put the house? You want to move it?"

"Nope. Guess again." Before Abilene could explain, Sabine caught up with them on the beach.

"I have a showing in fifteen minutes." Sabine held her lower back. "Four doors down. Some Hollywood couple in town for filming. They like Savannah so much they want to live here. Lots of million-dollar homes facing the same view as yours."

"Seriously?" Lars perked up.

"It's Savannah. Celebrities come and go." Abilene slipped into her sandals. "We don't bother them, and they try to blend in with the locals."

Lars's shoulders sagged again. "Bet their houses are not dilapidated like ours."

"Not to worry, Lars," Abilene said. "We have a plan."

"We do?" Lars's dimples formed again.

"I'll let you two hash it out," Sabine interjected. "If we're set for Friday morning, I'll see you at my office, say around ten o'clock?"

"Sounds good. We'll be there." Abilene smiled. Boy, did they have some construction news for Sabine and Tobias.

CHAPTER THIRTY

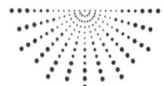

*I*t rained for days the next week, and all of Abilene's outdoor classes were cancelled.

Abilene was happy that she could work indoors at Simon's Gallery to make up for her pay deficit, but she was not happy that it had come at Simon's expense. It turned out he didn't have allergies. It had been a bad cold, and now he had bronchitis. His wife, Xian, had banned him from working for a week until he regained his strength.

For that reason, Abilene was getting paid this week.

Sitting at the reception desk of the art gallery, listening to the thunder outside and watching tourists with wet shoes stomp through the art gallery while waiting for the rain to subside, Abilene began thinking of her next series of paintings.

She liked the income from the sales of her paintings though she was surprised that Lars had bought her *Riverboat.* Nobody wanted her *Hutchinson Island* speckled with blue cows chewing cud on green grass. Sigh. Simon had hinted that his patrons preferred more traditional paintings of the local area.

She was thinking it was easy money, when the front door opened and in walked her past.

She didn't have to say a word. He had spotted her. Slung over a shoulder was a messenger bag that looked like something heavy was in it. One of his sculptures, perhaps.

"Abilene." His voice was deep, dark, quiet. It had always been. Once upon a time that voice had stirred something in her, but now it meant nothing.

"Winton, you cleaned up."

Winton scratched his chin. "Yeah. Got tired of the bushy beard."

"Was it bushy?"

"In the last two years it was."

Two years. It had been that long.

"Is Simon in?" Winton kept coming closer until the only thing dividing him from Abilene was the four-foot-wide counter. "I finished the sculpture I promised him."

"He's sick at home. Won't be in all week. You could leave it here for him, if you like."

"I'd rather give it to him myself. I don't want it to be accidentally sold." Something caught his attention. He walked past Abilene and went straight to a wall where one of Abilene's paintings was hung.

It was the Tybee Island Light Station. The striped black-and-white lighthouse rose into a dark sky.

Winton was the reason she had wanted the watercolor painting sold.

"The list price is cheap." Winton seemed miffed. "This was our painting. Why are you selling it?"

"Not *our* painting, Winton. I painted it myself."

"It must mean something if you kept it for three years before you decided to sell it."

"I didn't get around to it."

"Or you didn't mean the goodbye."

"I meant it." Abilene had thought their parting had been mutual. Winton wanted out of Savannah. She wanted to stay in Savannah perpetually. "It's been two years. It's over. Time to move on."

"Time to move on from what?" The question came from a third, unexpected voice. Lars didn't smile. His hands were in the pockets of his cargo shorts.

Abilene wondered how long he had been standing there, watching them, listening.

Abilene kept her voice cool. "Hey, Lars. We were talking about my lighthouse painting."

They both watched Winton squint at the price tag. "I'd pay more for that."

Winton walked back to Abilene, as if oblivious to Lars. "You know what, Abby? I'm starting a new teaching job at SCAD this fall. I can afford this. I'll take that lighthouse painting."

"Why?" Abilene asked, to which Lars raised his eyebrows.

"I was there when you painted it."

Now Lars shot darts of *What's going on?* at Abilene.

"Lars, this is Winton Pace, my—uh, old classmate at SCAD," Abilene said.

"I'm her ex-boyfriend." Winton stood eye to eye with Lars. "And you are?"

"Lars Cargill, her current fiancé and future husband."

"Oh." Winton dropped his hand. "I'm too late."

"Looks like it," Lars snapped.

Abilene had to break the stare-down. "Cash or credit, Winton?"

"Credit." He handed her one of the many cards in his wallet.

Abilene turned to Lars. "Would you be so kind

as to get the ladder from the storeroom so we can take down the painting?"

Lars didn't move.

"Okay. You check him out, and I'll get the ladder."

"I'll get the ladder." Lars went down the hallway.

"Why are you back in Savannah?" Abilene asked as Winton swiped his card. "There are plenty of teaching jobs elsewhere."

"I can't get a job anywhere else, Abby—"

"Stop calling me that."

"You let me call you that when we were together." He stared at her ring. "That's a pretty ring. When were you engaged?"

"Just last week."

"When's the big day?"

"We haven't set a date."

"So there's hope for me?"

"None whatsoever." Abilene dug into her tote bag underneath the table, for her travel mug. She placed it on the table. "You can also have that back since you drew it. You'd have to wash out the coffee at the bottom of the mug though. It's dried out since this morning."

"You kept the mug."

"It's insulated. But I don't want it anymore, and I don't want to throw it out. Thought you might like to have it back."

"If I hadn't shown up today, would you have given it to me?"

"I would've sent it to the thrift shop."

"A finality. It's really over between us." He reached for the mug tentatively.

The metallic sound of ladder parts clattering came down the hallway. Lars put it down in front of the sold painting. "If she says it's over, it's over."

"Sounds like it." Winton opened his messenger bag to put away the travel mug. Next to it was something wrapped in clear bubble wrap and silver duct tape.

He placed it on the counter. "That's what I want Simon to sell for me. Do you have a pair of scissors?"

Abilene did.

Winton cut through the duct tape. Then the bubble wrap. Something bronze and heavy was inside. Winton lifted it onto the counter.

~

The bronze sculpture was of Abilene reading a book on the couch, with Bradley the cat napping on her tummy. Only those who had gone to her house knew that was her favorite couch. The details were impeccable in the foot-long sculpture.

Lars felt his hair rise on his arms.

It was too close for comfort.

A stroke of jealousy hit him.

"It took me two years to make that," Winton declared proudly. "I just finished it a couple of months ago, but I couldn't get time off work to come here."

Two years? It didn't sit well with Lars that Winton, the ex-boyfriend, had been thinking of Abilene for the last two years.

"Well?" Abilene asked Lars.

"Well what?"

"What he made." Abilene lifted the bronze figurine and handed it to Lars.

It was heavy.

"I think it looks like a lot of hard work has gone into it." Lars was all businesslike.

"Yeah." Winton raised his voice. "Two years of my spare time."

"How much are you selling it for?" Abilene asked Winton.

He named a price. It was high.

"Let me text Simon." Abilene found her iPhone. She took a photograph of the bronze statue and sent it to Simon.

Next thing they knew, the gallery phone rang,

and Winton was on it, negotiating pricing with Simon.

Abilene walked around Winton and stood very close to Lars. Her eyes were questioning.

"We should let Simon handle the purchase," Lars whispered before she could say anything.

"I don't want the gallery to have it. That's a figurine of Bradley and me," Abilene whispered back. "If I buy it, will you be okay with it?"

The last thing Lars wanted in their future house, upcoming marriage, and life together was a figurine of Abilene made by her ex-boyfriend. Then again, it was Abilene on her old couch. When they moved to their new house, that setting would be gone.

And besides, it does have Bradley on it.

"I suppose I'm quite fond of His Royal Catness."

"And Bradley is fond of you."

"All right. I don't see the harm."

"Thank you!" Abilene wrapped her arms around Lars's neck.

Right then and there in the middle of Simon's Gallery, with people moving around them, Abilene planted a longing kiss on Lars's lips.

And because Lars thought Winton was watching them, he let her go on and on.

CHAPTER THIRTY-ONE

o accommodate the busy schedules of the Duprees, Modipes, Cargills, and everyone else who claimed a spot on their family trees, Abilene and Lars ended up pushing and shoving and squeezing their engagement party into that one Saturday on Labor Day weekend so that Grandma Dupree's many great-grandchildren—and Abilene's many first, second, and third cousins— could attend the event without missing too much school and work.

Somehow, due to cancellations and last-minute regrets, Abilene had counted just four people shy of the upper limit that the riverboat could accommodate. Pastor Flores was happy to hear that they wouldn't run afoul of the fire marshal.

One hour before the dinner party, Abilene and Nadine were in the ladies' parlor. Nadine was all nerves.

Abilene felt nothing but peace in her heart. God's peace.

"What would your mom say?" Nadine bit her nails.

"Dad's talking to her about it, probably as we speak." Abilene fixed her own hair. Nadine was no help.

"I'm a planner and scheduler, and I don't see it coming together." Nadine paced back and forth in the small room.

"What's not coming together?"

"This." Nadine's fingers poked the air. "Whose bright idea was it?"

"Lars and I came up with it together."

"And Pastor Flores, of all people. I cannot believe he agreed to it."

"We've been doing premarital counseling with him since July." Abilene put away her hairbrush. She zipped up her cosmetics bag. "We signed up for the couples' Sunday School class. That's plenty, don't you think?"

"If you didn't have to demolish your new house and rebuild, wouldn't your schedule be different from this?"

Abilene nodded. She remembered that meeting with Sabine and Tobias. They had concurred with her and Lars that it would be better to start over. "They're demolishing the house tomorrow, and construction begins next week. We're on track."

Nadine stopped pacing. "Six months. Can't they build a new house sooner? They do it in one month or less on TV."

"We're not on TV." Abilene pointed to the clock on the wall. "Have to change now."

"Sure. I'll stand guard so Lars doesn't come in."

"I'm not worried about him. He's probably talking to his brother."

"His brother, Colm? He's kinda cute." Nadine seemed to catch herself. "Your brother's kinda cute too."

Abilene rolled her eyes. "Dante is spoken for. Sort of."

"Sort of? Hmm..."

Abilene pointed to the clock again. "Could you make sure nobody tries to get in here? Especially Mom."

"Sure thing. Do you think Dante and I... Or Colm and I..."

Abilene shut the door in Nadine's face as nicely and quietly as she could.

Half an hour later, Abilene wore no veil, no

sequins, no train. She had on a simple white lace column dress that she had found at a store the week before. She prayed away her nervousness as she stepped toward the back entrance.

When Dad walked her into the dining room and the string quintet changed its tune, not everyone knew it was time to stand up. It was a big surprise to many.

In front of the room, Pastor Flores and Lars stepped on stage, as if this were all impromptu.

Abilene walked by Mom and squeezed her hand. Mom burst into tears, and Abilene knew then that she had accepted it.

Sitting at the same table, Grandma Dupree was beaming with joy so bright Abilene thought it was going to take out the chandeliers above. No doubt Grandma was thinking about how to mail everyone a hot sauce favor package by Monday.

"I thought this is an engagement party," someone said.

"Was," another corrected him. "It's a wedding now."

Now.

Wedding.

Abilene's brief walk to the front of the dining room was over before the quintet finished playing *Canon in D*. And the man who had stepped into her painting and then into her life now came forward to receive her.

Lars took her hand and drew her to himself, and throughout the entire marriage ceremony, his eyes never left hers nor did his hand let hers go.

CHAPTER THIRTY-TWO

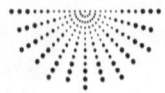

*S*even months later, Lars was still holding Abilene's hand every opportunity he had. He smiled into her eyes as they finished breakfast on the second-floor wraparound porch of their new plantation-style oceanfront home.

Abilene was glad that they had set the house thirty feet back from where the old dilapidated house had been. That spot now was covered by returning dunes.

Every now and then, she looked into the distance to watch pelicans flying south over the Tybee Island shoreline. Sometimes they could see porpoises rising out of the Atlantic Ocean but not this April morning.

The winter cold had left the coast, and Abilene

could feel and smell sneak peeks of the southern spring and summer.

Pretty soon the azaleas they'd planted in the front yard would complete their blooms, and tourists would flock to Tybee and Savannah. Until then, she and the other locals, including Lars now, had the island and riverside to themselves.

Like many other early mornings they had risen together to watch the sunrise, this morning was typical Tybee in April. The sun rose through many hues, and the ocean cheered. The sky was clear, and the day was nothing short of beautiful.

Lars offered Abilene more coffee. He'd brewed it himself, and Abilene was proud of his skill in grinding the beans to just the proper granular sizes before brewing these *perfect* cups of coffee.

Lars leaned back in his glider. "This is my kind of space. I'm glad we made this porch big."

"I love it here too."

"With all due respect, I'm glad we moved out of your old hole in the wall."

"Bradley and I liked it there." Abilene turned toward her cat—their cat—sitting on another patio glider. "Didn't we, Bradley?"

Apparently the cat didn't care. He slept on.

"Your old apartment was a little crowded for three," Lars said.

"Cozy."

"It's cozy here too, Abilene."

"I'll probably agree with that once we unpack all those moving boxes."

Lars groaned.

Bradley perked up his ears. He eased to his legs and leapt off the glider, strutting about until he found a spot where sunshine was warming the floorboards.

He plopped down on the floor and went back to sleep.

"I wasn't sure how he was going to adjust to this new place, but there's way more sunshine here for him to nap in." Abilene smiled.

"Thank God. I was afraid we'd have to move back into your old place."

"Look at the bright side. It was small enough to vacuum everywhere in ten minutes."

"I could do it in five now." Lars reached for Abilene. "We're still in our pajamas. Let's go back to bed."

"Can't. We have a meeting at nine o'clock."

"I almost forgot."

"You did forget. I just reminded you."

"Glad you did, Abilene. I think the gallery is going places."

"But first we have to move it to a high-traffic zone." A souvenir shop going out of business across the street from the Rousakis Riverfront Plaza was not unusual. But the business owner's decision to do a short sale at this time when Lars and Abilene were free to do a new project was a gift from God. If the building had been available two months before, they could not have purchased it, since they had been busy funding the construction of this new home.

"If all goes well, we could move the gallery in May or June and be ready for the peak summer season."

"May." Lars quieted. "We met last May."

"Has it been a year?"

"God has been good to us, Abilene."

"He's still good, you know."

"Yep, but I'm contented with what He has already done."

"There's more."

"How could there be more? My heart is full, Abilene."

"Make room in there for a little Dupree-Cargill." Abilene waited patiently for Lars to react.

He seemed stunned more than anything. "W-when?"

"This morning while you were making coffee. It's positive."

"I mean, when can we expect..." He waved his hands about. "You know..."

Abilene chuckled. "No idea. At most nine

months from now, I suppose, but Mom has said I was a late baby."

Lars stretched out his fingers one by one. "A winter baby. Four months after our first wedding anniversary."

"I guess we couldn't wait."

Lars was at the edge of his seat. "Call your GYN now."

"The front desk doesn't answer until eight. It's barely seven thirty."

"Half an hour. I'll remind you." Lars programmed it into his iPhone.

They sat there sipping coffee in silence for a while. Abilene spied Lars smiling. She wondered if their baby would have dimples like his.

"That explains your craving for fudge all week..." Lars jumped up. "Wow. Unbelievable."

"I'm happy too."

"I love you, Abilene." Lars pulled her to her feet, and hugged her, as gently as he could, as if mommy and baby were fragile. "God provides!"

"Yes, He does."

Abilene tried not to step on Bradley's tail. The cat was oblivious to the celebration.

Lars planted kisses on Abilene's forehead and chin and everywhere. "Now my heart overflows."

"Mine too, Lars. Mine too."

DEAR READER:

I hope you enjoyed the story of Lars and Abilene. The next book in the Savannah Sweethearts collection is *Cherish You So*, in which we meet Abilene's paraplegic brother, Dante Dupree, the future CEO of the Hot Dupree hot sauce empire. Is the handsome billionaire too hot for Abilene's friend, Nadine Saylor, to handle?

Cherish You So (Savannah Sweethearts Book 5)
JanThompson.com/cherish

READ A FREE EBOOK!

Set in Georgia, South Carolina, and Tennessee, this Christian romance tells the story of art gallery archivist Sheryl Breckenridge and world-famous sculptor Winton Pace.

Time for Me (A Vacation Sweethearts Prequel)
JanThompson.com/time-free

JOIN MY BOOK NEWS MAILING LIST

Subscribe to my mailing list to receive updates on the books that I have written, am writing, and will be writing. You don't want to miss surprise book sales and special announcements. Be the first to know about my new book releases.

Jan Thompson's Book News Mailing List:
JanThompson.com/newsletter

PLEASE WRITE A REVIEW

Thank you for reading *Draw You Near*. If you would like to leave a review, please follow this link to get to the retailers that list this book.

Draw You Near (Savannah Sweethearts Book 4)
JanThompson.com/draw

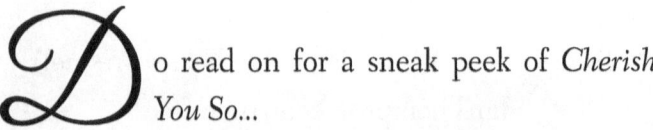 o read on for a sneak peek of *Cherish You So...*

THE NEXT BOOK IS CHERISH YOU SO

SAVANNAH SWEETHEARTS BOOK 5

Having come to terms with his disability, business empire heir Dante Dupree has it all, but Nadine Saylor is too busy to be impressed with his accolades, and too busy to fall in love. Yet, love keeps knocking on her door...

Cherish You So is Book 5 in *USA Today* bestselling author Jan Thompson's Savannah Sweethearts series of sweet, clean, and wholesome multiethnic contemporary Christian beach romance celebrating faith, hope, and love in Jesus Christ.

DANTE'S DREAM...

Billionaire bachelor Dante Dupree has arrived. Managing his paraplegia, he now has a state-of-the-art wheelchair to handle his disability, and a new private jet to take him across the world to buy up smaller companies for his family's Hot Dupree hot sauce empire.

And the best news yet for his career: he has been handpicked to be the next CEO of Hot Dupree, and he's going to inherit a fifth of the multi-billion-dollar family fortune.

He has it all.

At the end of an international business trip, Dante stops in Savannah for merger talks and to visit his pregnant sister, Abilene, now married and living on the beach.

Exuberant and on top of his game, single and free, the center of attention among ladies, and recently voted one of the top ten most eligible young billionaires in the world, self-confident Dante suddenly finds himself in a predicament he cannot solve: he's in love.

But he can't get her attention.

She is not impressed at all with his accolades.

NADINE'S NORMS...

Nadine Saylor is busy, busy, busy.

Her job as a virtual assistant to clients traveling through six or seven time zones keeps her on her toes around the clock.

The last thing she needs right now is Dante Dupree flinging signals and invitations at her, even though he did look handsome in his Lagerfeld tuxedo at his sister's wedding eleven months ago.

Nadine keeps telling herself that her calendar is full. There's no room for romance.

Dante can go find someone else to be his Flavor of the Month.

When one of Dante's professional problems intersects with Nadine's personal predicament, they find themselves thrown together to sort out these chapters of their lives.

Does Nadine accept Dante's offer?

Does Dante see Nadine as therapy?

Or are they mistaken?

Shouldn't they find strength in Jesus Christ, who saved their souls?

And has God put them together in this place for such a time as this?

∼

For book news, sign up for Jan's mailing list:
JanThompson.com/newsletter

Cherish You So (Savannah Sweethearts Book 5)
JanThompson.com/cherish

Savannah Sweethearts
JanThompson.com/savannah

Continue reading for a sneak peek of *Cherish You So...*

CHERISH YOU SO CHAPTER 1
SNEAK PEEK

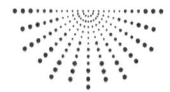

*N*adine Saylor spotted a striped, light-beige tail sticking out of the patch of sea oats. "Bradley!"

The cat ignored her. He continued to chew on the stalks swaying in the summer morning.

Beyond the dunes, a light breeze flitted across

Tybee Island, empty at this hour save for residents out and about, jogging or walking.

The day was calm.

But Nadine was not.

"You're going to get sick and throw up all over the place again. You know that. Bradley, come here!"

Nadine stepped closer but didn't leave the sand next to the boardwalk. The sea oats were a protected species, but the law against stomping all over them apparently didn't apply to cats.

Bradley moved farther away from her.

"Come on. I don't have all day." Nadine shook the plastic bag of cat treats in her hand, a poor substitute for natural green leaves. "Come here!"

"Coming!" A male voice resounded over the wash of waves from the Atlantic Ocean.

Nadine spun around—if it was possible on the shifting sand beneath her feet. Her sandals and toes dug into the sand.

Coming over the meandering boardwalk from the beach, Dante Dupree waved at her with one hand as the other pushed one of the hand rims of his wheelchair so casually that it looked like he was heading toward her in slow motion.

His curly hair, much like his sister's, shook in the Atlantic wind. Behind him were the sun and surf, another August day. He looked so fit and so athletic and oh so handso—

Banish the thought!

Nadine blinked before she stared too long at Dante's long arms flexing in the morning sunlight.

Dante was smiling like this was the best day of his life.

"Hi, Nadine." He came to a stop near her. "Need some help?"

He remembers my name.

"Hi, Dante." Saying his name was...interesting.

Here was Dante Dupree, one of the guys whom Nadine had thought she might like to go out with.

Once upon a time, that was, until she had found out that he dated numerous women here, there, and everywhere.

Forget about it.

Abilene had told Nadine that those women were dates, nothing serious.

Still, the perception of it bothered Nadine.

I want a gentleman, someone I don't have to hide from Mom and Dad.

Besides, I'm looking for character, not charm.

Nadine straightened up.

No reason to make this personal. Just because Abilene had been her best friend—well, until she got married—it didn't mean that the gesture extended to her older brother.

"I didn't know you were out here," Nadine said.

The last time she had seen Dante was at Abilene's wedding back in September. Dante had a flashy date with him, someone who looked like a million-dollar model.

Unlike me.

Dull, uninspiring me.

"Well, you were busy chasing after a cat. I heard you call his name the entire time I was over there." Dante pointed toward the end of the boardwalk. "Too bad the boardwalk doesn't extend far enough."

"Wouldn't that ruin the beach?" Nadine asked.

"I guess."

"Where are your all-terrain wheels?"

"This is all I have." Dante tapped the armrests with the base of his palms.

"Then it's your loss. You know that the Tybee sand is compacted. You could ride a bike on it."

"I live in the landlocked suburbs. I don't need an all-terrain wheelchair. Besides, I don't visit my sister that often. Well, not as often as I should."

Nadine glanced the other way at Abilene's beach house. "Nice house, isn't it?"

"They seem to like it out here," Dante said.

"You're not a beach person? You know, sun, surf, ocean?"

"No." Dante stopped smiling.

His voice was so clipped that it startled Nadine. "Uh, I'm sorry?"

"Don't worry about it. An old memory. Nothing to do with you."

"Well, good." Nadine glanced at her watch. "Anyway, Abilene said you'd be in town, but I didn't know you had already arrived. When did you fly in?"

"I'm two days early, but that's the way to succeed in life, right? Be ahead of the game." Dante lifted his sunglasses, resting them atop his head.

"Game? Life is not a game." Nadine stood where she was, staring at his steel-colored eyes. They looked...cold.

"Who says it is?" Dante lifted his eyebrows.

"You just did."

"I did?"

"Yes, I heard you."

Dante shrugged. "Figure of speech."

"Every word matters, you know," Nadine said. "God holds us accountable for what comes out of our mouths."

"What about forgiveness?"

"That too. But I'm thinking more of sowing and reaping. Action and consequences."

Whoa.

Nadine had no idea how those words had come

out of her mouth. All those years of sitting in church seemed to be paying off.

She wondered how much wiser she could be if she had spent more time in God's Word every day.

Ah... So much to do, so little time. Her clients demanded so much of her.

So tired.

So exhausted.

Nadine sighed. Too loudly, perhaps.

Dante tipped his head slightly. Smiled. "Some unresolved issues there?"

"What do you mean?"

"You've gone philosophical all of a sudden. That long, silent pause." Dante waved his hands at her. "I can see right clear through it. And here I am, thinking all you're trying to do is retrieve Abilene's cat from destroying the sea oats."

"Cat? Uh-oh." Nadine spun around. "Bradley, where are you?"

She paced back and forth, shaking the treat bag again. It was a useless exercise.

Abilene's cat was nowhere to be found.

"No. No. No." Nadine's heart sank. "What am I going to tell Abilene when she comes home from work?"

Dante chuckled. His wheelchair inched toward the edge of the boardwalk.

He was only a few feet away from Nadine.

Too close!

Nadine lost her train of thought.

Cherish You So (Savannah Sweethearts Book 5):
JanThompson.com/cherish

More Information about Savannah Sweethearts:
JanThompson.com/savannah

READ A FREE EBOOK IN THE SAME STORY WORLD

Set in Georgia, South Carolina, and Tennessee, this clean and wholesome Christian romance tells the story of art gallery archivist Sheryl Breckenridge and world-famous sculptor Winton Pace. Read this ebook for free!

Time for Me (A Vacation Sweethearts Prequel)

JanThompson.com/time-free

ACKNOWLEDGMENTS

Many thanks to my Georgia Press publishing team for keeping up with my writing schedule.

I appreciate author Heather Day Gilbert for copyediting this book, and copyeditor Dori Harrell and proofreader Lenda Selph for proofreading it. Thank you, ladies!

I am grateful to God for my husband and son for their support and encouragement. I also thank God for my parents and my three brothers for my happy and memorable childhood. I'll always remember my beloved mother and my late father for having instilled in me the love of reading and writing from a very early age. I miss my father here on earth, but I will see him again in heaven someday.

Most of all, I am eternally thankful to my Lord and Savior, Jesus Christ, who died on the cross to save me from my sins and rose again from the grave to give me eternal life. Without Him, I can write nothing (John 15:5).

Jan Thompson
John 3:16

BOOKS BY JAN THOMPSON

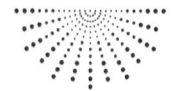

CONTEMPORARY CHRISTIAN CITY,
COASTAL, AND BEACH ROMANCE

Seaside Chapel (7 Books)
JanThompson.com/seaside
Savannah Sweethearts (12 Books)
JanThompson.com/savannah
Vacation Sweethearts (8 Books)
JanThompson.com/vacation

CHRISTIAN ROMANTIC SUSPENSE AND
NEAR-FUTURE TECHNOTHRILLERS

Protector Sweethearts (6 Books)

JanThompson.com/protector

Defender Sweethearts (6 Books)

JanThompson.com/defender

Binary Hackers (4 Books)

JanThompson.com/binary

Subscribe to Jan Thompson's mailing list:
JanThompson.com/newsletter

SEASIDE CHAPEL

Welcome to *USA Today* bestselling author Jan Thompson's Seaside Chapel Christian beach romance series. These novels are set on real-life St. Simon's Island, Georgia—a beach town where history is all around and the future is a moment away—and the neighboring fictitious Seaside Island, where the rich and famous live.

Savor the small-town atmosphere and the warm southern beaches of St. Simon's Island and the idyllic Golden Isles along the Atlantic Ocean. Enjoy the music of the orchestra and hymns of the church, and hang out with our Christian friends who attend Seaside Chapel, a little church by the sea known for its beach weddings and fair share of love and life.

As these Christians grow in their knowledge and understanding of God, they are tested in their spiritual maturity, their love lives, and their relationships with others. Share their heartaches and healing, and cheer them on as they celebrate faith, family, and friends.

- Book 0 (Prequel): *His Surprise Proposal*
- Book 1: *His Longing Heart*
- Book 2: *His Wake-Up Call*
- Book 3: *His Morning Kiss*
- Book 4: *His Quiet Serenade*
- Book 5: *His Waiting Love*
- Book 6: *His Beach Retreat*

For more information about Seaside Chapel:
JanThompson.com/seaside

SAVANNAH SWEETHEARTS

Welcome to the new south! From *USA Today* bestselling author Jan Thompson come these clean and wholesome, sweet and inspirational Christian romances set on the romantic beaches of Tybee Island and in the coastal town of Savannah, Georgia. Meet a group of multiracial and multiethnic churchgoing Christians who love the Lord, work hard in their careers, and seek God's will for their love lives. Against a backdrop of ocean, sand, and sun, these inspirational romances showcase aspects of the human need for God and for one another. Have some tea, settle in a comfortable reading chair, and enjoy these sweet celebrations of faith, hope, and love in Jesus Christ.

- Book 1: *Ask You Later* (Artist Romance)

- Book 2: *Know You More* (Multiracial Romance)
- Book 3: *Tell You Soon* (Asian-American Romance with Suspense)
- Book 4: *Draw You Near* (International Romance)
- Book 5: *Cherish You So* (Wheelchair Billionaire Romance)
- Book 6: *Walk You There* (Old-Meets-New Tour Guide Romance)
- Book 7: *Love You Always* (Romance with Suspense)
- Book 8: *Kiss You Now* (Multiracial Romance)
- Book 9: *Find You Again* (Multiracial Romance)
- Book 10: *Wish You Joy* (Christmas-Themed Romance)
- Book 11: *Call You Home* (Deaf Chef Romance)
- Book 12: *Let You Go* (Asian-American Romance with Suspense)

For more information about Savannah Sweethearts:
JanThompson.com/savannah

VACATION SWEETHEARTS

Travel with our friends from Savannah, Georgia, to the coast and to the mountains. Cheer them on as they celebrate the immeasurable grace and undeserved mercy of God through Jesus Christ.

The Vacation Sweethearts novels are a spin-off of Jan's Savannah Sweethearts series, and fans will recognize familiar faces from Riverside Chapel, a church in the coastal city of Savannah, Georgia. In fact, we might even visit the beach town of Tybee Island from time to time to visit old friends and beloved families...

- Book 0 (Prequel): *Time for Me*
- Book 1: *Smile for Me* (International Romance)

- Book 2: *Reach for Me* (Romance with Suspense)
- Book 3: *Wait for Me* (Romance with Suspense)
- Book 4: *Look for Me* (Romance with Suspense)
- Book 5: *Pray for Me* (International Romance)
- Book 6: *Care for Me* (Small Mountain Town Romance)
- Book 7: *Cheer for Me* (International Romance)

~

Read *Time for Me* (Prequel) for free:
JanThompson.com/time-free

For more information about Vacation Sweethearts:
JanThompson.com/vacation

PROTECTOR SWEETHEARTS

Private investigator Helen Hu and her associates specialize in searching for missing persons and hunting for lost treasures. Join them in their adventure suspense around the world in *USA Today* bestselling author Jan Thompson's Protector Sweethearts, a series of Christian Romantic Suspense with a side of mystery.

Protector Sweethearts is a spin-off of Savannah Sweethearts and Vacation Sweethearts.

- Book 1: *Once a Thief*
- Book 2: *Once a Hero*
- Book 3: *Once a Spy*
- Book 4: *Twice a Fighter*
- Book 5: *Twice a Convict*
- Book 6: *Twice a Soldier*

For more information about Protector Sweethearts:
JanThompson.com/protector

DEFENDER SWEETHEARTS

Defender Sweethearts is a sister series to the Protector Sweethearts Christian romantic suspense collection. While the heroes in Protector Sweethearts search for lost treasures and lost people, the Defender Sweethearts novels focus on protecting the helpless and hopeless. The main characters in Defender Sweethearts come from the supporting cast in Protector Sweethearts.

- Book 1: *Never a Traitor*
- Book 2: *Never a Hostage*
- Book 3: *Never a Fugitive*
- Book 4: *Always a Maverick*
- Book 5: *Always a Champion*
- Book 6: *Always a Guardian*

For more information about Defender Sweethearts:
JanThompson.com/defender

BINARY HACKERS

Like more suspense with your Christian romance? Like to read suspense thrillers? If you're looking for clean near-future romantic suspense without compromising the Christian faith, these books are for you.

From *USA Today* bestselling author Jan Thompson come these inspirational near-future cyberthrillers combining technothriller and romance, starting with Binary Hackers that feature computer specialists living at the edge of cyberspace, where they have to juggle being law-abiding truth-telling Christians while carrying out their assignments by any and all means possible.

The Binary Hackers series is set in the same story world as Jan's other books, and characters from the other series may make cameo appearances in this series and vice versa.

- Book 1: *Zero Sum*
- Book 2: *Zero Day*
- Book 3: *Zero Base*
- Book 4: *Zero Trust*

For more information about Binary Hackers:
JanThompson.com/binary

ABOUT JAN THOMPSON

USA Today bestselling author Jan Thompson writes clean and wholesome contemporary Christian romance with elements of women's fiction, Christian romantic suspense with an air of mystery, and inspirational international thrillers with threads of sweet Christian romance. Jan's books are for readers who love inspiring stories of faith, hope, and love in Jesus Christ.

Raised on a tropical island in the eastern hemisphere, Jan now lives and writes in the western hemisphere. Her international background gives her a unique multicultural and multiracial perspective to her novels and books. The island has never left her, and she reminisces about beach life in her beach romance novels.

When Jan is not busy writing small-town stories, she writes big-city romantic suspense and international technothrillers, a nod to her previous career in computer science. She weaves technology with human interests, reflecting the current and future digital world. And romance. There's always romance.

Beyond the printed page, Jan is a wife, mother, family scribe, avid reader, occasional artist, erstwhile pianist, and chief of staff to the family cat.

Find out more about Jan Thompson:
JanThompson.com

Subscribe to Jan's book news mailing list:
JanThompson.com/newsletter

For God so loved the world
that He gave His only begotten Son,
that whoever believes in Him
should not perish
but have everlasting life.
—John 3:16